CATHY
WILLIAMS
Beyond All Reason

Harlequin Books

TORONTO • NEW YORK • LONDON
AMSTERDAM • PARIS • SYDNEY • HAMBURG
STOCKHOLM • ATHENS • TOKYO • MILAN
MADRID • WARSAW • BUDAPEST • AUCKLAND

ISBN 0-373-11829-5

BEYOND ALL REASON

First North American Publication 1996.

Copyright © 1995 by Cathy Williams.

This edition published by arrangement with Harlequin Books S.A.

® and TM are trademarks of the publisher. Trademarks indicated with
® are registered in the United States Patent and Trademark Office, the
Canadian Trade Marks Office and in other countries.

Printed in U.S.A.

CHAPTER ONE

As soon as Abigail walked into her office, she knew that it was going to be a bad day.

She had had hardly any sleep at all the night before, had slept through her alarm clock and had had to rush about her small flat trying to dress and eat breakfast at the same time, and then, on top of all that, she had missed her bus to work and had had to engage in full-scale battle with three million other commuters on the Underground. Of course, she was late, and the note on her desk, with its bold, black writing telling her to 'See Me', didn't fill her with a sense of eager anticipation. She looked at her boss's door with a sigh, took a deep breath and knocked.

'Yes!'

Abigail pushed open the door and stepped in.

Ross Anderson was sitting behind his desk. He looked up as she entered and stared at her, frowning.

'Where have you been?' he demanded. 'I told you to come in at eight and it's now——' he looked at his watch as if he wanted to remind himself of the time which, she thought, was a joke because she could guarantee that he knew precisely how late she was, and simply wanted to ram the point home in that endearing way of his '—half-past nine.' He sat back in his swivel chair and clasped his hands behind his head in an attitude of, Well, I'm waiting and be quick about it.

Abigail looked at him evenly. After one and a half years, Ross Anderson still had the power to make her feel uncomfortable. Those lean, dark, predatory good

looks might charm the rest of the female sex into coy, blushing smiles and fluttering eyelashes, but she had always stoutly refused to let them do anything for her. She had had enough of good looks to last her a lifetime.

She answered him now in her usual calm, unhurried voice, 'I'm sorry, I had a late night.'

'You had a late night?' He sounded incredulous, as if she had uttered some startling, incredible revelation of epic proportions. His black eyes skimmed over her with the insulting thoroughness which had not been on display for a very long time, not since she had informed him coldly that if he couldn't respect her then he could look elsewhere for a personal assistant. She had just started working for him and had still been licking wounds and rebuilding defences, and had most certainly not been in the market for a flirtatious boss with more than his fair share of charm. In fact, if only he had known it, that glimpse of sexy charm so apparent when he had interviewed her had all but sent her skittering away in search of another job.

'Doing what?' he asked.

'That's none of your business. What did you want to see me about? I typed those letters you wanted and left them on your desk, and I've rearranged your meeting with Mr Grafton for next Wednesday.'

'It damn well is my business,' he retorted, ignoring most of what she had said, 'when your late nights intrude on your working time.'

He stood up and walked around to the front of his desk, and then perched on the edge of it. Standing, he towered over her and she had to resist the temptation to walk right out of the room and back into the relative sanctuary of her own little office.

'I don't make a habit of arriving late,' she defended.

'Where were you last night?'

She lowered her eyes and said with reluctance, 'I went out for dinner with a friend.'

'Well, well, well. No need to act as though you're confessing under torture. That only arouses curiosity. What friend?'

The amused curiosity in his voice made her head snap up in sudden irritation.

'I don't believe you know him, so there would be no point in telling you his name.'

'Him? His name? A man?' He smiled and that infuriated her even more.

As far as Ross Anderson was concerned, she was an open book. Unexciting Abigail Palmer with her shoulder-length brown hair, always neatly combed back, and her calm grey eyes. True he had once tried to use that easy charm of his on her, but she had firmly stamped on that, and he had shrugged with raised eyebrows. It wouldn't have bothered him. Charm, as far as he was concerned, oiled the wheels of daily existence, but if she refused to play that game then she doubted that he really cared, just so long as she produced the level of dedication to her work that he wanted. Which was one hundred and ten per cent.

No doubt he had proceeded to assume that she was a quiet little mouse with an existence to match. How dared she have an outside life of which he was not aware? Least of all one that involved a man?

After a few weeks, when they had become used to one another, and ground rules had been tacitly accepted, she had caught him looking at her once or twice, a question in his eyes, trying to piece her together, just as he tried to piece everyone together, and she had always smilingly kept him at bay, and after a while, as they slipped into a comfortable working routine, he had given up.

She knew that he would not have been in the least puzzled if she had a vibrant social life, or if there were

a string of ardent lovers waiting in the foyer for her when
she was ready to leave. No, what puzzled him was her
remoteness. She had discovered very quickly that remoteness was not a quality which was much in evidence
in the women he dated. He was accustomed to beautiful,
self-confident, outgoing types who laughed loudly, flirted
like mad and generally made no effort to disguise what
they wanted.

She knew that she was nothing like that and could
never have been like that if she had taken a ten-year
acting course in how to be a successful extrovert. Her
personality had been too successfully moulded by her
mother from an early age. How could you go through
life, through all those formative years, having scorn
poured on your efforts, without creating a wall of silent
self-defence around yourself and a tendency to conceal
what there was no need to reveal?

Experiences, especially of the bitter variety, left their
acrid mark, and, where her background left off, her last
disastrous brush with passion took up.

'Well?' he prompted. 'You never told me that there
was a man in your life.'

Abigail blinked. 'No,' she murmured, pretending to
give the matter some thought. 'You're quite right, I
didn't.'

'And you're not about to.'

Not if I can help it, she thought.

'I don't see any point in bringing my personal life to
work,' she said by way of explanation.

'I've noticed. Admirable, I'm sure, just so long as that
personal life which you don't bring to work doesn't entail
your getting here late.'

Abigail clenched her fists in impotent anger. Wasn't
this just like Ross Anderson? Normally she would have
bitten her tongue and kept silent, but she was in no mood
to be heroic this morning. There was a lot on her mind

and all she really wanted was to submerge herself in her work and forget those niggling worries which, for the past three months, always seemed to be there in the background, somewhere, threatening to pounce.

'I never complain about your personal life being brought into work,' she muttered under her breath.

'What?' His voice was deadly calm and she flushed uneasily. She hadn't expected him to hear that remark—she might have guessed that he had the ears of a hawk.

'Nothing,' she said. 'I'm sorry. I'm awfully tired, and,' she added for good measure, 'I have a headache.'

He stood up and stared down at her and she looked back at him nervously.

'Not too tired to function, I hope?' he asked sarcastically. 'You're no good to me if you're going to spend the day drooping around like some damned wilting flower.' He strode over to his desk and began rummaging through the open files, and she watched him reluctantly. There was no doubt that he commanded attention. Under the tailored suit, his body was hard and very masculine. She had been to several client functions with him, and she had seen the way women were drawn to him, fascinated by his lazy charm and mesmeric sex appeal. He spun round and she raised her eyes to his, reaching out to take the stack of files.

'I've attached some work in these which you'll need to have typed by this afternoon,' he said, flickering through each one while she watched with her mind miles away. 'There are three reports which need some additional information slotting in. Hello!' he bellowed. 'Is there life here? Are you listening to a word I'm saying?'

Abigail jumped and looked up at him guiltily. 'Of course I am.'

'What the hell did you get up to last night with the man with no name, anyway?' he asked and she didn't

say anything. 'No need to answer that one,' he murmured in a silky voice, 'I get the picture.'

'I'm sure you find it very amusing to speculate on my private life, Mr Anderson,' she said coolly, taking the files from him because it gave her something to do with her hands, 'but not all of us live in the fast lane like yourself.'

He laughed and folded his arms. 'And what does that cryptic little remark mean?' he drawled.

I won't let him fluster me, she thought. She had learnt how to ride through his more provocative remarks with a sense of humour, without him seeing how addled they sometimes made her, and she looked up at him now, her face composed.

'It means whatever you take it to mean, Mr Anderson,' she said politely.

'I take it to mean that you didn't spend last night making passionate love with the man with no name.'

'His name is Martin Redman!' she snapped, immediately regretting her outburst because that only seemed to fuel his amusement. 'Now, if you'll excuse me, I'll get to my desk so that I can begin working on these files.'

'Hurry off, then,' he said, his mouth twitching at the corners, and much as she would have liked to flounce out of his office, she walked out in as calm and dignified a fashion as she could muster. Sometimes, she thought, sitting at her desk and switching on her computer terminal, sometimes I wish I could ram these files down his throat. That would go a long way to wiping the amused smile off his face!

Good old Fate. Trust it to have landed her this job eighteen months ago. At the time she had been working for a small firm of lawyers. Too small a firm, she later realised. She was the only secretary there, and her normal caution when it came to the opposite sex had gradually

been eroded by the late nights she had found herself working. Ellis Fitzmerton had been one of her bosses, and she had gradually begun doing more and more work for him, knowing him in that casual but intimate way that was possible between two people who spent a great deal of working time together. There had been a drift towards take-away meals when overtime was necessary, often in an office empty but for the two of them. Legal talk had shifted to personal talk. The memory of it still made her flush. In retrospect, she couldn't believe how stupid she had been. Ellis Fitzmerton was slick, good-looking, appealing. Little by little common sense had given way to an empathy she had never invited; and when, late one night, over a stack of files, of all stupid things, he had leant forward to kiss her, she had thrown caution to the winds and returned his passion. It had been an error of judgement which had lived to haunt her.

She shut the memory out and began typing the stack of letters, her fingers flying expertly over the keyboard, and she barely glanced up when the connecting door opened and he swept into the room, his black coat over one arm.

'Feeling less tired now?' he asked, propping himself with his hands on her desk, and she stopped what she was doing to look up at him. Up close, he was dauntingly handsome. His features were angular and the darkness of his hair and eyes gave a brooding impression that could be intimidating and vaguely cruel. She had trained herself never to respond to his unsettling good looks and she looked at him placidly.

'Much less, thank you. When shall I expect you back from your meeting with Mr Robinson?' She briefly scanned her desk diary and informed him that he was seeing one of the marketing people later on in the afternoon.

'Don't worry,' he said, his black eyebrows curving upwards, 'I won't be running behind schedule, so you needn't fear that you'll be called upon to do any overtime tonight.'

She snapped shut the diary. 'Oh good,' she murmured, gathering together her sense of humour which had threatened to desert her earlier on, 'I am so relieved to hear that. You know how eagerly I wait for five o'clock every evening, bag in hand, jacket on, feet poised to flee and join the general stampede of clock-watchers.'

'Oh, all right. I take back that crack.' He stood up. 'Tell Janet to have all the sales figures ready this afternoon, I don't intend to waste my time standing around while she rummages through her folder in a complete flap.'

'I'll tell her,' Abigail said. Poor Janet. Ross Anderson had a knack for making people nervous, and Janet was no exception. The last time she had a meeting with him, she made the mistake of forgetting some of her brief and had had to endure his barely contained impatience while she attempted to sort through her things for the relevant information.

'What the hell's the matter with you?' Ross had asked her afterwards, when Janet had finally left the office, with an expression of relief on her face, and Abigail had looked down at her notepad where she had been jotting down the relevant points of the meeting.

'Nothing,' she had said, which had made him scowl darkly at her.

'She should have made sure that everything was prepared before she came in here.'

'She's human.'

'I'm human,' he had pointed out irritably, 'but that doesn't mean that I drift in and out of my meetings in a state of semi-chaos.'

Abigail had looked up at him wryly, and he had snapped, with a dark flush, that he was not obliged to justify his behaviour to her anyway.

He stood up now, glanced down at his watch and said that she could expect him some time after lunch.

As usual, after he left, the office seemed peculiarly empty and very restful. She worked steadily for the next two hours and then sat back with a little sigh of weariness.

She would have her lunch now, she decided, a yoghurt and some fruit, and she would try not to spend the next half-hour analysing her relationship with Martin. She enjoyed his company, he enjoyed hers and they felt comfortable with one another.

She peeled off the top of the carton and relaxed back in her chair, swivelling it around so that she was staring out of the window, although the view was hardly inspiring. Grey sky, grey tops of buildings, grey strip of road in between the buildings, and to the right an isolated, lonely green blob which constituted the nearest park. Sometimes she wished that she had never chosen London as a place to live, but it offered the best jobs and in a way she had become quite accustomed to its crowded streets and frenetic pace. Every time her mother travelled down from Shropshire to visit, she made a point of telling her daughter how silly it was to live in London when she was a country girl at heart, a description that always left Abigail feeling that by country girl she meant boring yokel. And that in itself was enough to guarantee that she stayed put, right where she was, in her tiny flat in North London.

She had just finished her yoghurt when the office door swung open and Abigail looked up to find herself staring into two very blue eyes.

'May I help you?' she asked, and for a while the other woman didn't answer. She simply prowled around the

office, the bright blue eyes scanning everything, until
she found herself opposite Abigail's desk.

'You are Ross's little secretary, I take it?' Her voice
was as cold as her eyes. 'I'm Fiona St Paul. Perhaps
Ross has mentioned me.'

'No, I'm afraid he hasn't.'

Since the other woman had no compunction about
observing her, Abigail returned the scrutiny with one of
her own. Fiona St Paul was very tall, very slender, with
the smooth, sleek lines of a model. Her blonde hair was
cropped short and her skin had the porcelain fairness
that hinted of Scandinavian blood. Her voice, however,
was very upper-crust English.

'No,' she said coolly, 'I don't suppose he would have.
Not to you, anyway. Can you fetch him for me?'

'Mr Anderson isn't in at the moment, I'm afraid,'
Abigail said without too much regret.

'Well, when will he be back?' The scarlet lips were
pursed with irritation.

'Some time this afternoon.'

'Some time? *Some time*? Could you be more specific
than that?'

Abigail tried to smile politely and failed. 'No,' she
said bluntly, 'I cannot be more specific than that.
Perhaps I could get him to call you when he returns.'

'Yes, my dear, you most certainly could.' She sat down
on the chair opposite the desk and crossed her legs el-
egantly. She was wearing a pale blue silk suit and a thick,
camel-coloured coat. 'And could you call me a taxi? It's
absolutely *tipping* down outside and I can't quite face
standing out there trying to hail one.' She inspected her
nails, which were the same shade of scarlet as the lipstick.

This, Abigail felt very tempted to point out, is not
part of my little secretarial duties, but she picked up the
receiver and after a brief conversation managed to secure
a taxi to arrive outside the building immediately.

'Jolly good,' Fiona said, standing up and brushing down her skirt. 'And don't forget to tell Ross that I dropped by and that I'll see him tonight for the theatre.' With that, she left the office, leaving behind her a waft of expensive perfume.

No wonder, Abigail thought, that he had had no hesitation in informing her that he would not be running late today. She gazed at the computer terminal and wondered at which stage this particular romance was. She had not heard mention of Fiona St Paul before but that didn't mean that she hadn't been on the scene for at least a couple of months. She certainly ran true to type as far as Ross's women were concerned. Tall, elegant, self-assured. She switched on the computer terminal and thought of Martin.

'Just your type,' her mother had gushed when she had first met him four months ago.

'Ordinary, you mean?' she had asked drily, because her mother's implied insults no longer drove her into paroxysms of self-conscious embarrassment the way they once had as a teenager.

'Nice and stable,' her mother had returned. 'You don't want to lose your head over a man you wouldn't be able to keep. Remember that last fiasco of yours.'

It had been a mistake telling her mother about Ellis. She had immediately delivered a lecture on the impossibility of an ordinary girl handling someone like him. Never mind that she had never actually met Ellis Fitzmerton. That, according to her mother, had been a minor technical detail, and certainly not enough to stop her announcing her views on the subject.

Nice, stable Martin, Abigail thought now. She was very fond of him and when she had accepted his marriage proposal one week ago, she had done so safe in the knowledge that he would be a good husband, someone on whom she could rely. They had only been

seeing each other for a matter of six months, but she
knew that she felt relaxed and comfortable with him and
that was what love was about, she was certain. He had
been such a pleasant change from the suave, deceitful
Ellis with his promises and declarations which had lasted
all of six weeks, until the girlfriend she never knew he
had returned from her glamour trip round the world,
bronzed, beautiful and ready to resume where she had
left off. Oh, the declarations had certainly gone by the
board then, she thought bitterly. Love? Marriage? He
had looked at her white face with wide-eyed incredulity.
'You must have misread the signals, sweetie.' He had
shaken his head sadly, ruefully, pained at the thought
that he might have given her the wrong ideas.

Martin was far too decent a human being ever to play
games like that. She frowned and felt that little niggling
worry which she immediately swept to the back of her
mind.

It was after four when Ross swept back into the office.
He paused by her desk and she reeled off his telephone
messages, then she said, glancing down at the typed
letters, 'By the way, you had a visitor. A woman by the
name of Fiona St Paul. She said that you'd know who
she was.'

She thought of the other woman, that chic elegance
wrapped up in expensive designer clothes, every nail
manicured, every strand of hair firmly in place, and she
felt an uncustomary jolt of jealousy. How ridiculous,
she thought, with an uneasy inward laugh.

'What did she want?' Ross asked, slinging his coat
over the spare chair and shrugging out of his jacket.

'She expected to find you here,' Abigail said. 'She was
disappointed that you weren't in.'

'Get her on the phone for me, would you?' he said
by way of response. 'She works at Sotheby's.' He strode
through to his office and Abigail looked at his retreating

back with dislike. He rarely involved her in anything to do with his women. She knew of their existence because of the theatre tickets she booked for two, the intimate meals she reserved in expensive restaurants, the flowers she occasionally ordered, but beyond that they mostly remained a mystery. Several she had met in passing, and from them she had deduced that he was attracted to physical perfection. Now she got Fiona on the phone with a certain amount of unwarranted resentment and, as they connected, she heard his voice down the line, warm, full of sexy charm.

He certainly can turn it on, she thought, replacing the receiver softly. Even when he stormed through the office, subjecting her to his evil moods, she could tell that underneath that terseness lay the sort of lazy charm that most women would find hard to resist.

Ellis Fitzmerton might have been a bitter pill, but he had served his purpose. He had immunised her against folly, and that was why she had excelled in this job. Ross Anderson could not distract her.

Janet arrived for her meeting five minutes early, and spent the time chatting to Abigail while nervously contemplating the door.

'He won't eat you,' Abigail said, following the line of her gaze.

'No,' Janet agreed, 'but he still scares me half to death most of the time.' And what could Abigail say to that when she fully understood the line of thought?

'At least,' Ross said to her one hour later, after Janet had left his office and was safely on her way back to peace on the sixth floor, with her own easy-going marketing boss, 'she came prepared this time.' He was getting ready to go, slipping on his jacket, looking at her absent-mindedly as he did so.

'You terrify her,' Abigail said bluntly, and he stopped what he was doing and looked at her, surprised.

'Do I? Why?'

'Why do you think? You're unpredictable.'

His black brows met in a frown. 'I'm not sure I like that description of myself.' He sat on the edge of her desk and began rolling down his sleeves, buttoning them at the wrists. 'I don't terrify you,' he observed.

'I'm accustomed to you, perhaps.'

This was beginning to veer off their normal routine conversation and she felt suddenly awkward.

'You've grown accustomed to my face?' he murmured, sensing her mood with amusement. 'Something like that?'

'Something like that, I suppose,' she replied, not looking at him, walking across to collect her coat from the stand in the corner of the room. She turned to find him staring at her, his dark eyes unreadable.

'I suppose I've grown quite accustomed to yours as well,' he murmured, making no move to leave so that she was forced to stand by him, hovering, her hands stuck into the pockets of her coat. 'But that doesn't mean that I know you any the better.'

She didn't care for the way his eyes were boring into her and she certainly didn't know what sort of response to make to that, so she remained where she was, silent.

When the silence eventually became unbearable, she said, in a burst of discomfort, 'What play are you going to see tonight?'

'Changing the subject?' Ross asked, eyeing her. 'Why are you so cagey about your personal life?'

'I'm not cagey about my personal life,' she said, horrified to find that her mouth was dry and her brain felt as though it was seizing up. She was used to dealing with him when he was in a filthy temper, so why was she feeling like this when he was being nice? Because, a little voice told her, nice is dangerous when it comes to a man like Ross Anderson.

'No? Then how is it that you never let on that you were seeing a man? Not even in passing?'

'Because...' she stammered, going red.

'Because it's none of my business?' He stood up and slipped on his jacket.

'I never really gave it much thought,' she said with an attempt to be casual. 'Gosh, is that the time? I must get going.'

'Dinner date?'

'Something like that,' she said and he bit out angrily, 'There you go. Dodging a simple question, acting as though the minute you say anything revealing about yourself you'll find yourself in the firing line.'

She shot him a placating smile which was supposed to remind him that she was, after all, just his personal assistant, and he gave her a long, sardonic stare. 'Careful you don't fall, Abby,' he murmured, and she looked at him, bewildered. 'You're backtracking so quickly that you might just lose your balance.'

He moved towards the door and held it open to her.

'Musical,' he said succinctly into her ear. 'A much safer topic, isn't it? Fiona and I are going to see a musical in the West End and then we shall probably have dinner somewhere.' He pressed the button on the lift and turned his attention back to her. 'What about you? Where is your boyfriend taking you to dinner?'

Was it her imagination or was there laughter in his voice every time he mentioned Martin?

'Actually,' she offered with reluctance, 'we're having dinner at my place tonight.' She glanced at him out of the corner of her eye and then said, because he would find out sooner or later anyway, 'It's something of an engagement party, as a matter of fact. Just relatives and a few friends.'

Ross stared at her as though she had suddenly sprouted three heads and announced that she was from another planet.

'Well,' she said defensively, 'I would have told you! It's not some great secret. I just never thought that you'd be interested.'

The lift arrived and she stepped in with a feeling of relief. She had her head averted, but she was acutely aware that he was still staring at her. What right did he have to make her feel guilty simply because she happened to be a very private person, who preferred keeping things to herself? Nonetheless, she felt a slow flush creeping up her cheeks.

'So you're getting engaged to this Martin person,' he mused. 'You don't seem to be overjoyed and excited at the prospect.'

The lift doors opened on to the ground floor and she stepped out. With some surprise she realised that she was perspiring slightly.

'Of course I am,' she said more hotly than his remark warranted. 'I'm very excited about the whole thing.'

'What's he like?'

They were walking across the huge reception hall now, but not fast enough as far as she was concerned. Ross Anderson, she knew from experience, was the persistent sort. She had seen it in everything he did. He grappled with problems until they were sorted out to his satisfaction, and he could be ruthlessly single-minded in pursuing his targets. It was one of the reasons why his company, in times of recession, had continued to do well, to expand. Publishing was a volatile beast at the best of times. She knew, as everyone in the company did, that he had inherited an ailing firm from his father, and had then proceeded to drag it kicking and screaming into the twentieth century, until it was now one of the largest in the country, with branches operating throughout Europe.

Quite simply, Ross Anderson had taken the company by the throat and had brought it to heel.

He hadn't achieved that by being a sensitive flower. She eyed the approaching glass doors with zeal.

She had managed to ignore his question and was about to launch herself through the revolving doors, to freedom, when she felt the warm pressure of his hand on her elbow, and she sprang back, alarmed.

'What are you doing?' she asked, and he said very softly into her ear,

'From your reaction, not what you think.'

'Very funny,' she muttered between her teeth.

'I was simply going to ask you whether you had time for a quick drink. To celebrate your engagement.'

'No.' She tired to water down the abruptness of her answer with a smile. 'I really must get home so that I can prepare some food for tonight.'

'How many people have you invited?' he asked blandly, his hand still disconcertingly on her elbow.

'Not many. I would have asked you along,' she explained, 'but...'

'But you're a firm believer in not mixing business with pleasure. I know. I got the message three days after you joined the company.'

She looked at him, startled.

'Surprised I remember?' he asked, and she shrugged.

'Not when I think about it. You have the memory of an elephant. Sometimes I think you must have the entire collection of the *Encyclopedia Britannica* up there, roving about in your head.'

'Shall I take it as a compliment?'

'If you like.' Her voice was casual, distracted even though her heart was doing some pretty odd things inside her and she couldn't for the life of her imagine what had prompted that observation.

'You know, sometimes I think I almost prefer Mrs Fulbright, your predecessor, whose lifelong ambition was to reveal the maximum about herself in the minimum amount of time.'

That hurt. 'You could always ask me to resign,' she said, her grey eyes angry.

'Don't be stupid,' he snapped impatiently, 'I'm not asking you to do anything of the sort. I'm merely trying to make a point.'

'I can't help the way that I am, Mr Anderson,' Abigail said inaudibly, 'I...'

'Yes?' Their eyes met and the breath caught in her throat.

'Nothing. Look, I really must be dashing off.' She took a step backwards, knowing from his grim expression that the subconscious retreat had registered with him. 'Do have a nice time at the play tonight,' she said, while he continued to stare at her tersely. 'I shall be in bright and early in the morning.' She was running out of friendly parting words and it suddenly occurred to her that she was under no obligation to make excuses for her personality. She was his employee, and one who did a damn good job. She was conscientious, hardworking and trustworthy and that was all that mattered, wasn't it?

She turned away abruptly and walked through the revolving doors, and the sudden cold winter air outside was like a balm.

As luck would have it, she had missed her bus again, but this time she hardly noticed the press of bodies on the Underground. Her mind was too busy sorting through the extraordinary atmosphere that had sprung up between herself and Ross. She had never felt so uncomfortable with him before. True, from time to time in the past she had caught him looking at her, but this

was the first time that she had felt so entirely the target of his overwhelming personality, and it had alarmed her.

It wouldn't do to forget Ellis and the way he had ignored her the minute his girlfriend had reappeared on the scene. She had so nearly given in to him, slept with him, she had been so caught up in the frenzy of never before experienced desire.

She thought of Ross, and for a moment the image that sprang back at her of his implacable, hard good looks was so sexual that she sucked in her breath with shock. Had she actually wondered what it would be like to have those strong hands on her body? No, she told herself uneasily. He had just managed to creep under her skin a little with his damn inquisition, but that was all.

The train disgorged her at her stop and she walked the remainder of the distance back to her flat, feeling calmer as she began to look at things in perspective. He had unnerved her. She was not accustomed to being unnerved. After eighteen years of living with her mother, she had learnt how to maintain a steady, unshakeable front, and the fact that that front had been rattled, for once, had taken her aback.

It would never have happened, she decided, letting herself into her flat and immediately heading for the kitchen to make herself a cup of coffee, if she wasn't already in a fragile frame of mind. She had spent most of the night awake, thinking about Martin's proposal, about the engagement party which would formally seal it, wondering whether she had done the right thing. She had convinced herself that her head was right when it said yes, and if her heart was being a bit belligerent, then that would settle in time. It just so happened that Ross had decided to cross-examine her when she was mentally not up to it.

She looked at her watch, gulped down the remainder of the coffee, and then spent that next hour putting the finishing touches to the food which she had prepared over the weekend and stored in the freezer.

She found herself hurriedly taking a shower, then changing into a slim-fitting silk dress in blues and purples, which she had bought months ago but had never got around to wearing because whenever she tried it on all she could see was the revealing depth of the neckline, and that immediately made her wonder what on earth had possessed her to buy it in the first place.

After thirty minutes of rapid dressing, she stood in front of the full-length mirror in the bedroom and looked at her reflection with a critical eye.

Not bad, she decided. No abundance of voluptuous curves, but a neat figure nevertheless. She had applied some blusher to her cheeks, so her skin did not look as pale as it was wont to do, and her eye-shadow made the most of her eyes, which she personally considered to be her best feature.

When the doorbell rang, she drew in her breath, crossed her fingers that her mother wouldn't do anything to antagonise Martin's parents and that the handful of friends they had invited would get along, and went to answer the door.

CHAPTER TWO

'ALL right. Out with it. What's eating you?'

'Nothing's eating me.' Abigail stared down at her notepad and thought that something was eating her all right, and whatever it was it was making a great meal of it ever since the evening before when Ross and Fiona, unexpected, uninvited and unwanted, had shown up at what was supposed to be a small, intimate celebration party.

Everything had been going just fine until they turned up. There had been no embarrassing pauses in the conversation, no snide remarks from anyone, lots of congratulations, lots of food, and her mother had been on best behaviour, even if Martin's parents, a rather timid couple, had seemed occasionally overwhelmed by her presence. That had been expected. Her mother had a tendency to be overwhelming at the best of times.

'Then why,' Ross continued with a hint of impatience, 'have you been sitting there for the past half-hour looking as though the world's caved in? Have you been listening to a word I've been dictating?'

'Of course I have.' She held up her notepad which was full of scribbled writing and tried not to fling it at him.

'It's because I turned up at that engagement party of yours last night, isn't it?'

'Why did you?' Their eyes met but she didn't look away. Why bother to pretend that she didn't have a clue what he was talking about?

25

He shrugged and looked at her. 'Curiosity, I guess. If you hadn't been so secretive about the whole thing, I probably wouldn't have.'

Curiosity. She digested the word with something approaching dislike.

His sudden appearance in her flat had elicited varying reactions from the assembled guests. Martin's parents, with a certain amount of obtuse naïveté, had assumed that he had been invited, in the capacity of Abigail's boss. They had even made an effort to involve Fiona in conversation, seemingly not noticing the languid boredom on her face or the way her eyes skimmed derisively over the décor. Her own mother had viewed him with rather more suspicion, and Abigail had seen the twitching antennae with a sinking heart. More lectures to come on good-looking men and how they should be avoided at all costs; remember Ellis Fitzmerton. We don't want you making a fool of yourself over another boss, do we?

And of course Martin, who had never met Ross before, as if sensing unfair competition, had adopted an air of macho aggressiveness which had not sat well on his shoulders. Poor Martin. That, in some respects, had been the worst thing about Ross's unexpected arrival. He had stridden into the small sitting-room, with his bottles of expensive champagne, tall, commanding, sexy, and instantly everyone had seemed very dull in comparison. Including Martin.

'Come on.' He stood up, shoved his hands in his pockets and Abigail said, bewildered,

'Come on? Where? What are you doing?'

He had walked over to where she was sitting opposite him and proceeded to frogmarch her to the door, while she made ineffectual protesting noises.

'I'm taking you to the boardroom,' he said, pulling open the outer door and unceremoniously escorting her

out. 'Life's just too damned offputting with you in this kind of mood. Whatever little resentments you're nursing, you'll bloody well tell me about them over a cup of coffee.'

'No!' She tried to pull away, not liking the way his fingers burnt her skin. 'What about work? This is silly!'

He ignored the protests and continued to pull her along the corridor.

'Work can wait.'

They reached the boardroom and he pushed her in, slamming the door behind them.

'Now,' he said tightly, turning to face her with his arms folded, 'get it off your chest.'

He stood with his back to the door, staring at her, his black eyes glittering, and she gave him a weak smile.

'It won't work,' he informed her in a curt voice, and when she looked at him with a question in her eyes he continued tersely, 'that smile of yours. It won't work.'

'What smile of mine?' She smiled.

'That one. The placating one that you produce every time you're in an uncomfortable spot. The one that precedes a change in conversation.'

'I have no idea what you're talking about,' she muttered, looking away, and he said, moving towards her with his arms still folded,

'Oh yes, you do. You're fine just so long as work is involved but the minute I make any personal remark to you, however damned inoffensive, you throw me one of those smiles, edge away and take refuge behind the word processor, or the telephone, or that notepad of yours.' He whipped the notepad out of her fingers and she instantly felt bereft without it.

'Now sit down!' he barked, making her jump, and she sat down, following him warily with her eyes as he walked across to the coffee-machine and began fiddling with it. After a few minutes, and cursing under his breath, he

shot her a black look and said with disgust, 'The damn thing's broken.'

'It was working yesterday,' Abigail offered, and he scowled. 'Are you sure you know how to work it?'

'Of course I know how to work it,' he told her impatiently. 'It doesn't take a degree in metaphysics to work a blasted coffee-machine, does it?'

She got up and went across to the non-functioning coffee-machine, pressed a few buttons, and was rewarded by the familiar gurgling noises.

He looked at her with a disgruntled frown, as if she had been personally responsible for its previous lack of co-operation with him, and said under his breath, 'Pointlessly fiddly gadget. I suppose manufacturers think it's clever to make something simple as complicated as they can.'

'I suppose they do,' she agreed easily, feeling much more relaxed.

'And that's another thing!' he roared at her. 'Another trait of yours! Agreeing with everything I say if you think it's going to get me off your back!'

Abigail started to smile soothingly, and stopped in time. She made their cups of coffee and retreated back to the sanctuary of her chair. For a minute there, standing so close to him, she had felt her heart beating fast and her pulses racing, as if she had just finished running a marathon.

He sat down next to her and crossed his legs, his eyes speculative, trying to read inside her mind, to unearth what thoughts were flitting through her head. It filled her with a trace of alarm, because there were times when he had shown a distinct talent for doing just that, and it had always unnerved her.

'Why were you so put out last night? When you opened the front door and saw us standing there, your face was like a thundercloud.'

'I don't happen to like my private life intruded into on the grounds of curiosity!' she snapped. She had wondered why he had marched her along to the boardroom for coffee and a so-called chat when both could have been accomplished back in his office, but now she knew. He had brought her here to disorient her, to talk to her out of familiar surroundings, where he would have the clear advantage. In this silent, large boardroom, with its stark gleaming table and its array of chairs standing to attention around it, there was no easy flight behind familiar objects. And no distracting telephone calls which might have given her the opportunity to leave his office quietly when he was too busy talking to intervene. Here, there were just the two of them and her thumping heart.

'All right then, forget curiosity. I've known you for eighteen months. I came to extend my congratulations to you formally.'

She didn't believe a word of that and her look said as much.

'Dammit, Abby!' he bit out impatiently. 'You made it patently clear from the start that you weren't interested in a boss who was going to... to...'

'Flirt with me?' she offered with irony, and he glared at her.

'If you want to put it that way.'

'I'm not interested in that,' she said, hearing the bitterness creep into her voice and wiping it out before he could start making deductions.

'And I've tiptoed around you for long enough. Why did it make you so uncomfortable having me around?'

She flushed and looked away. Why had it? she wondered uneasily. He was just her boss, she thought. They worked well together and that was that.

'Your girlfriend was bored stiff,' she said, deflecting the unwelcome thought. 'She perched on the edge of her chair, looking as though she might catch something in-

fectious at any moment. How do you think it feels to have that at your engagement party?'

She glanced down at her finger, now sporting a discreet engagement ring, and felt a strange quiver of unreality. Suddenly things seemed to have happened very quickly, almost behind her back, when she hadn't been looking.

'Fiona can be tactless at times,' he admitted, 'but you still haven't answered my question.'

'I didn't like the thought of your barging in, if you must know, looking at us as if we were strange oddities.'

'What the hell do you think I am?' he said, his face hardening. 'Did you imagine that I came to sneer?'

She didn't answer and that seemed to make him angrier.

'I suppose not,' she conceded reluctantly, not daring to meet his eyes, 'but I'm just your secretary, after all. We don't exactly move in the same circles, do we?'

Watch out, Abby, a little voice warned her, you're beginning to sound bitter again.

She couldn't help it though, the shadow of Ellis Fitzmerton made that impossible. After he had broken off with her, he had explained in a phoney, gentle voice that had nothing to do with sympathy and everything to do with reminding her of her position, that she must have been suffering from delusions if she thought that they could have made anything out of their brief, albeit pleasant, relationship. And when she had seen his girlfriend, she had understood why. They may have drifted into something because of circumstance, but there was a dividing line between them that was insurmountable. He had reinforced the refrain that had played in her ears ever since she had been a young child. Them and us and ne'er the twain shall meet. Beauty, her mother had once told her, can jump all barriers, but you might as well be honest and face facts, you're no great beauty.

Ross gave her a long, intense stare, then said suddenly, 'Who was he?'

'Who?' Abigail stammered, going bright red, and clutching the seat of the chair to stop her hands from trembling.

'The man who filled your head with rubbish like that?'

'I don't know what you're talking about,' she said sharply. 'And I don't have to stay here a minute longer and listen to this!'

'Was it your mother, then?'

'What makes you say that?' At this point, every nerve in her body was jangling. This was the first time, she realised with panic, that he had ever managed to get any conversation between them on to an intimate footing and hold it there.

'She struck me,' he murmured thoughtfully, in a deceptively mild voice, 'as the sort of woman who doesn't mind thrusting her opinions on to other people, including her own daughter. That can be a disaster when it happens to a child, or an adolescent.'

He gave her a sidelong glance from under his lashes.

'She can be a bit domineering, I suppose,' Abigail admitted, only realising afterwards that she had fallen for a trap. He had given her a choice of talking either about a man or her mother, and she had chosen her mother when in fact, if she had been thinking straight, she would have seen that she was under no obligation to discuss either.

'This is stupid,' she said, fidgeting but not actually summoning up the courage to get up, 'sitting here, wasting time talking about nothing, when there's a pile of work back in the office waiting to get done.'

'We're not talking about nothing. Unless that's how you would describe your life.'

'And stop putting words into my mouth!'

Their eyes clashed and she felt a strange, giddy sensation overwhelm her.

'How long did your friends stay?' he asked, veering off at another tangent. He sipped his coffee and regarded her over the rim of the cup. Compelling. That more or less described him. His looks, his mind, everything about him compelled. Why else would she be sitting here being persuaded, against her will, to talk about herself?

'An hour or so after you left,' she said.

'Very nice girls,' he murmured, and she had the sneaking suspicion that he was leading up to something, though what, she couldn't quite figure out. 'Have you known them a long time?'

'Years. I grew up with Alice, in fact. I'm an only child and she was like a sister to me.'

'Down-to-earth, sensible girl,' he mused, leaning back in the chair, his long, lithe body dwarfing it.

'Yes, well, we all are,' Abigail said tartly. 'Reality isn't something you can escape from when you have to strive for every little foothold you gain in life.'

'That sounds like philosophising to me.'

'I guess it does,' she answered with a reluctant grin. 'I didn't lead a deprived existence, I always knew that there would be food on the table, but that luxuries were out of the question. Now,' she said briskly, 'have I answered all your questions? Do you feel that you now know me? Can we return to work?'

'There is all that paperwork on the takeovers to work through, isn't there?' he agreed, raising his eyebrows, as if only now giving that any thought at all.

'Yes, there is!' She didn't want to sound eager, but on the other hand she had no desire to continue their fraught conversation. In fact, she would have happily taken on a charging bull with her notepad if it would

have provided the necessary distraction from Ross's intimate probing.

'And you're right, there's a pile of paperwork waiting on my desk to be sifted. Usual stuff. Letters from clients, contracts that need signing, statements to look at. Routine things, but they do take up one's time.'

'Yes, they do!' she agreed lustily.

'But it can all wait, I think. At least until we have another cup of coffee.' He held out his cup with barely concealed amusement and she threw him a furious look.

Playing games. That was what it was all about, she thought, rapidly refilling his cup and handing it back to him. Games that had been initiated from curiosity. She hated games. She had always been a serious girl, with her feet firmly planted on the ground, and her head where it should be, not spinning somewhere in the clouds.

The only man who had ever played games with her had been Ellis, with his smooth patter. Had his games been initiated through curiosity as well? Or boredom? Or maybe they had been the effect of their enforced late nights alone in an empty office? Whatever, they had taught her a bitter lesson, and she felt a sweeping resentment that Ross was toying with her as well.

Martin was not a game-player. He took life seriously as well. She had a fleeting mental image of him. Pleasant-looking, with neatly combed brown hair and blue eyes. A thoroughly nice chap, as her friend Alice had whispered to her at some point during the engagement party.

She wondered, in a flash of sudden insight, whether she hadn't allowed herself to enter into a relationship with him because he was just so different from Ellis, because he was sincere at a time when sincerity was the one thing she desperately needed.

She had met him at a dinner party, where they had automatically paired off, being both single, and it had just developed from there. No heady passion, no thunder

and lightning, just a quiet, unfussy friendship between two people who shared similar interests. But would she have responded to him if that disastrous romance only months previously had not left such a sour taste in her mouth?

The thought confused her.

'The food was very good,' he mused, holding her gaze until the unsteadiness that she had been feeling since they had entered the boardroom threatened to take over completely. 'I never knew that you were such a good cook.'

Abigail sighed in resignation. 'You don't give up, do you?'

'Whatever do you mean?'

They both knew what she meant. He had broken through the carefully controlled barrier that had always separated her private life from her working life by turning up at that engagement party, and he wasn't about to desist until his perverse curiosity about her was satisfied.

'I'm not a bad cook,' she said. 'Why are you suddenly so interested?'

'What makes you think that I haven't been interested in you from the start?'

It was a curious way to answer her question and for a minute it threw her into speechless silence. Her mind flew back over the past eighteen months, and snippets of conversation between them resurfaced from the depths of her subconscious, like little eels wriggling free from the rocks under which they had been firmly buried.

She remembered times when he had asked her about herself, about what she did in the evenings, what movies she liked, whether she ever went to the theatre. And she could remember her responses with equal clarity. The uninformative, abrupt answers, the firm closing of any door between them that he might have been trying to open.

The rational side of her knew that it was stupid to let what had happened between her and Ellis affect the way she looked at the rest of the male sex, she knew that the constant erosive effects of her mother were a legacy she should leave behind. But she couldn't help herself. Ross Anderson, she had known from the very start, was precisely the sort of man she should steer clear of, and she had made sure that she listened to her head and obeyed its instructions.

He continued to stare at her in that unsettling way of his, until she said nervously, with a little laugh, 'Of course I did far too much food! There was an awful lot left over. I shall be eating cold chicken and beef in various guises until doomsday.'

'Sounds a dismal prospect,' he murmured softly, tracing the rim of the cup with one long finger.

'Do you do a lot of cooking?' she asked awkwardly, wondering when the inquisition would come to an end.

'Not if I can help it, no. In fact, I spend most of my eating time in various establishments. It suits me.'

'Sounds an unhealthy habit,' she said with a faint smile. 'You're probably lacking all the essential minerals and vitamins your body needs to grow.' It had been a nervous quip, but once she had said it she groaned inwardly at her clumsiness. What on earth had taken possession of her? Where was all the cool self-control that had been in evidence ever since she had started working for him?

'Do you think so?' he asked seriously enough, although there was something wickedly amused in his voice.

She kept her eyes firmly averted from his body.

'My mother was a great believer in eating up all one's greens,' she said by way of reply. 'I guess her constant reminders about carrots and eyesight and broccoli and strong bones must have stuck.' She tried a cheerful laugh.

'Anyway, I couldn't afford to eat out every night of the week even if I wanted to.'

'An unhealthy habit,' he agreed, 'as you said.' He looked down and idly rotated the coffee-cup in his hand. 'Your boyfriend didn't strike me as someone who craves expensive meals either.' He hardly looked as though her response to that observation was of paramount importance. His voice was casual, off-hand, speculative. Still, she felt her body stiffen. Wasn't it inevitable that he would drag poor Martin into the conversation? She frowned and wondered why she was now mentally referring to him as Poor Martin. Silly.

'In fact,' Ross was saying in the voice of someone who had rummaged through his mental database and unearthed some mildly interesting memory, 'I was subjected to quite a lecture on the shameful, profligate ways of the rich.'

Abigail didn't say anything but she gave an inward groan of despair. As soon as Ross had walked through the front door, capturing everyone's immediate attention, Martin had seen it his duty to jostle for attention, and his method had been to talk much louder than he usually did and to hold forth on subjects with perverse dogmatism. It had been a side to him which she hadn't seen before, but then again, she had never seen him in competition, however needless, with a man like Ross.

She had missed his lecture on the rich. She had, she thought, probably been clearing away the dishes and taking refuge in the kitchen. She could imagine it all too well, though. In fact, after all the guests had left, he had said to her in a disapproving voice, 'Overpowering man, your boss. I can't imagine working for someone like that, but then I guess he's got what it takes to run a company like his.' He had made that sound like a distasteful threat

but she had been too exhausted by then to pay a great deal of attention to what he was saying.

Martin had a managerial job in a computer company, and he was quite happy with that. His ambitions did not soar to dizzy heights and he was fond of telling her that his parents were perfectly content with their lives, and *they* never had a great deal of money to throw around. His father was a retired schoolteacher and his mother helped out on a part-time basis at a local flower shop.

'There's more to life than money,' she heard herself say stoutly. 'Anyway——' she glanced away from that hard-boned, intimidating face '—Martin's not usually so...so...' She searched around for the right phrase and finally said, 'Outspoken. He's a warm, generous person.' Her voice had risen slightly and the sudden lift of Ross's dark brows made her glare at him with irritation.

'I'm sure he is,' he replied as though her warm outburst had surprised him. 'After all, you're marrying the man.'

'And what exactly is that supposed to mean?' She stood up, flustered, not giving him time to respond. 'I really think we ought to be getting back to the office,' she said.

'And since when do the secretaries dictate the orders?' Ross enquired, with an edge of flint in his voice.

'I apologise,' she said calmly, breathing deeply to clear her head and restore her balance, 'but I refuse to be subjected further to this dissection of my private life.'

He looked as though he was about to debate that point, but in the end he shrugged his broad shoulders and stood up, reaching out to hand her her notepad.

'You'll be needing this,' he murmured with amusement, and their eyes met. To hide behind again, he might just as well have said, and she took it without rising to the bait.

Why did he have this effect on her? she wondered desperately. Why *did* he have this tight, strangling effect on her? Martin never did. They spent their time chatting, going for walks, and she never felt as if the world was closing in on her.

She put it down to dislike, and yet there were times when they worked so well together that she felt almost a mental bond with him. It was aggravating. Of course, she should never have accepted this job in the first place. She should have gone to work for some safe, fatherly figure with a receding hairline and a comfortable paunch. Someone whose presence didn't threaten her. She would have too, if the job description and the pay package hadn't been so irresistible.

They walked back to the office in silence. She could feel his presence alongside her, dark, oppressive, alarming.

'Rebecca was quite taken with that boss of yours,' Martin had said the night before. 'Began giggling and batting her eyelashes the minute he came through that door with that I'm-better-than-everyone-else air about him.' His voice had been laden with derision. 'Still, he's the sort of chap women fancy, I suppose. Bit too aggressive by half for you, though, I should think,' he had added, looking at her for confirmation, and she had agreed fervently, although her wayward mind had conjured up an image of Ross naked, in bed, his muscled body relaxed, his mouth curved into that cynical, charming smile, and she had forced the image away with angry recoil.

Now that wayward mind of hers was threatening to invade her calm again, and she resolutely thrust it back.

Ross went straight through to his office, expecting her to follow, which she did, breathing a sigh of relief as he returned his attention to work.

He ploughed through documents on his desk, leaning forward to explain to her what he wanted done, listing meetings that he wanted set up within the next fortnight. She kept her head bent, taking notes, nodding, watching the strong forearms, the dark hair curling over the gold metal band of his watch with stubborn fascination.

'These columns need updating,' he told her, his eyes flicking over the paper. 'The correct figures are attached at the back. You'll have to go through them and replace whatever needs replacing.'

She craned forward to see what he was talking about and he said impatiently, 'Come around the desk. You'll twist your neck in that position.'

'Yes, of course, Mr Anderson,' she said neutrally, moving around to stand behind him.

He had rolled the sleeves of his shirt to the elbows and she stole a surreptitious glance at his powerful forearms. She wished that she hadn't because immediately a disjointed thought rushed into her head: what had he and Fiona done last night? She imagined him caressing the tall, elegant blonde with those strong hands, and crossly shoved the unpleasant image to the back of her mind.

'Look,' he said, jabbing his finger at a row of black figures, 'here. These are last month's sales figures, which need replacing, but I want you to keep these graphs handy.' He sifted through to the graphs and she leant forward slightly to follow what he was saying, frowning and trying to puzzle out how she could update sixteen pages of information without having to redo the whole thing from top to bottom.

She peered forward, her eyes intent, and the silky cowl-necked shirt gaped to expose a tantalising glimpse of pale breasts restrained by the small cups of her lacy bra. She didn't notice. Her mind was busy trying to work out the complexities of the job in front of her. It was only when

she glanced away from the report that her eyes fell on what Ross had already observed, judging from the expression on his face.

He had turned the swivel chair so that he was directly facing her and there was a lazy grin on his lips. She straightened quickly and looked at him, forcing herself to meet his gleaming dark eyes.

He clasped his fingers together, challenging her to say something, which she didn't. His eyes drifted from hers and did a leisurely sweep of her body, resting briefly on her breasts, which hung heavy and aching under the stare. Her nipples pressed against the lacy material and she had to force herself not to surrender to the terrible, crazy thought of what it would feel like to have Ross touch them, with more than just his eyes.

What the hell was happening to her? Not even Ellis had ever awakened this depth of arousal in her. True, her body had willingly responded to his when he had made that first pass in the semi-darkness of his office, and true, over the ensuing weeks she had enjoyed their stolen caresses, the husky timbre of his voice as he had explored her body with his hands, sometimes at the most inappropriate moments, but what she felt now was so intense that she almost caught her breath.

She had thought that her fling with Ellis had been an aberration, a temporary insanity. Certainly one of the nice things about Martin was that he hadn't pushed her into sex. They were both content to kiss, but he had not frantically tried to get her into bed, and that had been a relief. Desire was no basis for a long-term relationship. She had found that out the hard way.

'I think I've got that,' she said coolly, moving back around to her chair and not looking at him.

He was still smiling in a way that made her want to hit him, and eventually she said crisply, 'And by the way, I still have that Haynes report to do. I had to phone

around several people to get the information you wanted and some of them weren't in when I called. I should have it ready and on your desk by this afternoon.'

'Very enterprising,' he said silkily. 'What would I do without you?'

'Find someone else, I expect,' Abigail returned neutrally.

'Easier said than done. But stupid speculating over a problem that doesn't exist, isn't it?'

She didn't say anything. She was remembering Martin's desire to start a family and the adjunct that when they did so she would leave work. At the time—and it had only been mentioned once—she had given it little thought, not wanting to immerse herself in details such as those when they weren't even married yet.

'Or does it?' he asked softly, reading her expression, and she went red. When she wasn't careful, when she wasn't guarding her expression, this man could see right through her, to what she was thinking. A dangerous skill. 'Married women usually lose interest in their jobs,' he murmured, picking up his fountain pen and thoughtfully twirling it with his long fingers. 'Their honeymoon seems to scramble their brains and they come back with their heads still in the clouds and their minds on children and nappies. You seem to have your head screwed on all right at the moment, despite the tired eyes and the late arrival yesterday, but——' he looked at her '—your lover strikes me as the sort of man who can't wait to get the little woman behind the kitchen sink. Am I right?'

CHAPTER THREE

ABIGAIL'S hand was still poised over her notepad. It was beginning to ache, and she lowered it.

The hard cold sunshine streamed in through the large glass panes and threw Ross's face into disturbing shadow so that she found it difficult to read his expression. Was he merely expressing curiosity or was he really worried that she was about to stack her papers neatly together on her desk and take her leave?

'I don't know what gives you that idea,' she stammered, and he stopped twirling the fountain pen in his fingers, putting it on the desk so that he could lean back in his chair, looking at her through his lashes.

'Isn't he?' he asked by way of response, and she felt like a butterfly pinned against the wall.

'These letters,' she suggested coaxingly, in an attempt to change the conversation, and his lips twisted into a crooked smile,

'Won't work, Abby,' he said softly, and she felt herself begin to bristle from head to toe. She didn't have to sit here and be cross-examined! Explaining her personal life to him wasn't part of her secretarial duties. She hadn't asked him to turn up on her doorstep the evening before, but he had anyway, and now he was acting as though the brief visit entitled him to make sweeping statements on her relationship with Martin. It was ludicrous!

'I understand that you might be worried about my leaving this job when I get married——' she began, and he cut in in a voice that took her by surprise,

'When? Has a date been set?'

'No, but engagements normally lead to weddings, don't they?' she said in a dulcet voice.

His jaw hardened, and he stood up, walking to the window to stare down. She could see the reflection of his face on the glass, the stiff line of his back. She saw it all with a sense of dismayed fascination.

'Of course he's not suited to you at all,' he informed her, not turning around, and she stood up, the notepad dropping to the ground. Her hands were trembling and she couldn't believe her ears.

'I beg your pardon?'

'You heard me.' He swung around to face her and his black, brilliant eyes swept over her from head to toe. 'If you marry that boy you'll be making the biggest mistake in your life.'

'He is not a boy!' was all she could find to say to that, which sounded utterly inadequate.

'He's way too pale, insignificant for you. You'd be bored to death within a year.'

'I don't believe that I'm hearing this! I don't think I asked for your opinion!'

'No, but you should be grateful for it. I'm saving you a lifetime of regret.'

He sat back down in the black chair, for all the world as though nothing had happened, as though he hadn't just behaved in the most arrogant, high-handed manner conceivable. She looked at him furiously.

'Oh, sit down,' he told her impatiently, and she made a choking sound. 'We have work to do, have you forgotten?'

'How dare you tell me how to run my life?' she bit out, sitting down with her hands pressed into her lap. 'What gives you the right?'

'I'm not telling you how to run your life,' he grated, 'I'm merely offering you advice.'

'When I want advice, I'll ask for it. Thank you!'

He shrugged in a gesture of dismissal, as though ready to move on to something else now that he had voiced his uninvited opinions, and she picked up the notepad from the floor, very tempted to hurl it at him.

'Right,' he said, staring down at the papers in front of him, and before she could utter another syllable he began dictating, his voice hard and rapid, the words flowing easily as he flicked through the stack of paperwork.

'You don't even know him,' Abigail said through gritted teeth, when there was a pause before he moved on to the next document, and he said easily, expecting her to return to the subject,

'I know enough. Don't tell me that you'd be content to play the suburban housewife with a weekly allowance and a handful of screaming children.'

'Lots of women do.'

'But not you. You have an inner fire, Abigail. It's there lurking just beneath the calm surface.'

'Thank you, Dr Anderson, for that valuable piece of insight. When can I expect your bill?'

He laughed. 'Point proved. I don't see that acid sense of humour going down at all well with the boyfriend.'

'His name is Martin. And you're never wrong, are you?'

'I try not to make a habit of it.' He began on the second letter and she stared down at the notepad, copying quickly as he spoke while her mind furiously tried to grapple with what he had just told her. Of course he didn't know Martin, didn't even know her, come to that, so as an onlooker he was highly unqualified to make sweeping generalisations about either of them. She knew that she should simply disregard every word he had just said, but anger tugged away at her, and as soon as he had stopped dictating she took up where she had left off.

'Martin and I are very fond of each other,' she said defensively, and he threw her an amused, mocking look.

'I'm very fond of my cleaner, but I wouldn't propose marrying her. So——' he looked at her with gleaming eyes '—very fond of each other, are you?'

'Yes, we are! I know that might not seem like a great deal to you, I know that that must seem the most boring thing on earth, but marriage is all about being fond of your partner.'

'Oh, is it?' He appeared to give this some thought, then he shook his head and drawled, 'And I always thought a hint of excitement was a good thing.'

She knew what he was up to, of course. He was trying to provoke a reaction in her, trying to antagonise her into saying something which would compromise herself. She knew his tactics. She had sat in enough high-level meetings with him and had seen that particular ploy in action. He would needle in that cool, cynical way of his until he got the reaction he wanted, then he would pounce. She stared with intense fascination at the little scribblings on her notepad and didn't reply.

'I've jotted some notes in the margins of this report you did a couple days ago,' he said, reaching across to slide it towards her, and she took it, still in silence.

'Martin can be very exciting,' she crossly heard herself say, 'not that it's any of your business.'

'Of course,' he murmured soothingly, and she wanted to hit him.

'He's a very warm, caring human being!' she expanded in a high, indignant voice, her face hot.

'I'm sure.' The black eyes held hers for a moment, then he lowered them but not before she saw the amused glitter in them. Ha, ha, she thought, hilarious. What a riot, affording me the wisdom of his great mind.

'Is that all?' she asked stiffly. 'May I leave now?'

He ignored her. 'He told me that he's looking forward to getting married, to settling down. He hopes to make it to accounts manager within the next two years. This was after he had delivered his informative lecture on the disgrace of being ambitious or having money.'

'You brought out the worst in him. Anyway, what's wrong with being an accounts manager? The world is full of very fulfilled accounts managers. You make it sound like a sin.' Worse, she thought, he made it sound boring, which no doubt was exactly what he had intended.

'A little dull, perhaps,' he mused, and she scowled. 'But to each their own, I suppose.' He stood up and looked at his watch, then began rolling down his shirt-sleeves, tugging his tie into position. 'I'll be with Jim Henderson until lunchtime. Expect me back around two.'

He slipped on his jacket and she walked towards the door, her body rigid, as if she had just undergone an ordeal by fire. She should never have risen to his bait, of course. A bit late in the day to realise that now, but she would know better next time, if there was a next time. She moved towards the door, frowning, but before she could leave he had moved alongside her. She felt his proximity with a jolt of alarm. Silly. She started to brush past him through the doorway, but he barred her retreat with his arm and she was forced to look up at him.

As her eyes met his, her mouth went dry and she felt giddy.

'You know,' he said thoughtfully, his voice husky, 'in that dress you wore, you looked ... sexy.'

The silence was deafening. In it she thought she could hear the rapid beat of her heart, could almost hear the racing of her pulses.

She couldn't think of a thing to say. Her mind had gone completely blank and she stared back at him, her pupils wide and dilated. What was going on here? Was

he flirting with her? It was a situation which had never arisen before, and because of that she had imagined herself immunised against his charm. Now she felt as though her head was stuffed with cotton-wool and it took a great deal of effort to reply with anything remotely resembling calm.

'It was my engagement party,' she said, her mouth aching. 'You wouldn't expect me to wear a suit, would you?'

'I have no idea what I would have expected,' he replied, staring down at her. His eyes weren't quite black, but they were very dark. She could see the flecks of brown in them, the black circle of iris, the long, thick eyelashes. 'But whatever it was, you surprised me. I'll bet your mother disapproved.'

She went pink. 'Of course not! Why on earth should she?' She had, of course.

'No reason. Just that she looks as though she might frown heavily upon her daughter in the role of sex siren.'

'Hardly that.' She managed what she hoped sounded like a laugh, but her body was screaming as though he had touched her intimately, even though he hadn't laid a finger on her. He didn't have to. He was one of those men who could touch with their eyes. She dragged her gaze away from him and swept the fall of hair from her face with an unsteady hand.

'You'll be late for your meeting.' Her voice was almost inaudible, but she thought that she had done very well by simply managing to say anything at all.

'So I might,' he agreed in a low, lazy voice, then his finger touched her neck, tracing the delicate ridges of her collarbone, down to the neat white lacy collar of her shirt. No further, but enough to make her breasts ache with awful arousal. She pulled back sharply and he laughed under his breath.

'Look after the fort,' he murmured, and she could feel his eyes on her without having to look. 'See you later.' With that he was gone, and as soon as the outer door had closed behind him she fell back against the wall, her body trembling all over as if she had ague. Gradually the wheels of her brain began churning into life again, but it was a while before she made it to her chair, to the cosy comfort of her computer.

The shock of what had just happened, which, she uneasily told herself, was precisely nothing, began to wear off and anger took its place. Anger that he had dared lecture to her on her life, anger that he had done his best to provoke an answering reaction from her, anger that he had had the audacity to flirt with her simply for the hell of it. Wasn't that why she could never be attracted to a man like him, even though she could look at him and understand why so many women were? He threatened with his very presence. He had managed to imply that Martin was dull, boring, tepid, but excitement was like living on the edge of a precipice, never knowing when you would go hurtling down to the rocks below. She was, she reflected, not an exciting person. She had never been an exciting person. A 'quiet little thing' was how her mother used to describe her to her friends, and what was wrong with that? Look at where so-called excitement had got her in the past. Oh, it hadn't broken her heart, nothing so dramatic as that, but it had given her a very illuminating and not to be repeated confrontation with mortification.

Let other people play their dangerous games of love: she would settle for placidity and contentment. And Martin.

She spent the morning half concentrating on her work, half berating herself for being distracted when she found herself unable to concentrate, but it was helpful not having Ross around. It gave her time to collect herself

together, and when he strode back into the office at two-thirty she could quite calmly look at him, hand him his messages, ask him how the meeting went, without revealing the slightest flicker of emotion.

After two days, she began to think that she had imagined everything. Had he really looked at her with that dark, mocking charm or had it been some kind of temporary illusion brought on by who knew what? She had been in a fragile state of mind after their conversation about Martin and she could understand how she might have over-reacted to some perfectly innocent compliment, some perfectly innocent gesture. She wasn't his type any more than he was hers, and they both knew that. That was one of the reasons why they had managed to work in such harmony from the start: because there had never been any sexual innuendo between them. Flirting was second nature to him. He had an abundance of masculine charm and he used it almost without thinking, but the minute he had seen that she wasn't interested he had backed off, because what he really wanted was a secretary who gave everything to her job, and, since that had been precisely what she had been looking for, they had found that strong common ground.

On the Tuesday afternoon, Martin phoned to tell her that he would collect her at her office next day instead of meeting her at her flat, because a meeting with one of his customers had cropped up at the last minute and couldn't be avoided.

'I shall have to work until at least six,' he grumbled down the line. 'Why can't people arrange meetings for sensible times, like ten in the morning?'

'We can always postpone it,' Abigail said, absent-mindedly re-reading what she had just typed on the screen in front of her. 'The film won't vanish for at least another month or so.'

'No,' Martin said a little aggressively. 'Why should I ruin my evening because of some damned meeting? I shall make sure it's wound up by six latest and I'll see you at your office around six-thirty. That should give us time to have a bite before we go to the cinema.'

'That sounds fine,' she said hurriedly as Ross pushed open the door and walked into the room. He looked at the telephone, then at her and paused to stand by her desk, perching on the edge while she abruptly told Martin that she had to go.

'I hope I haven't interrupted an important personal call,' he said in a barbed voice, and she sighed.

'No, of course not.'

'Boyfriend?'

This was the first mention of Martin for days and she looked at him warily.

'Yes.' She began printing the letter on the word processor, hoping that the irritating noise would encourage him to leave, but it didn't. He stayed right where he was, eyeing her while she busied herself collating the letter, and she eventually met his stare with reluctance.

His black hair was combed back, making the lines of his face appear harsher, more arrogant, and his eyes were lazy but watchful.

'Going somewhere?' he asked, and she thought she heard amusement in his tone.

'To the movies. Tomorrow evening. We usually go once a fortnight.'

'Creatures of habit,' he mused, and she clamped her teeth firmly together, determined not to let him get under her skin this time. 'I'll be out all day tomorrow,' he said briskly, standing up, taking the letter which she handed him and glancing quickly through it.

'Where?' She frowned, not recalling any all-day meetings in her diary, and he slid a sidelong look at her.

'Do I have to report all my actions to you?'

'I like to know where you are in case someone wants to get in touch with you.'

'How efficient. In that case, I'll be at home until around lunchtime, then at a private viewing at the Tate Gallery from three onwards. In other words——' he leaned towards her with his hands on her desk '—I shall be taking the day off for reasons of pleasure and not business.' He grinned and added, 'Do think twice about interrupting me at home. There's nothing worse for lovemaking than the sound of a telephone.'

He strode into his office, whistling, and Abigail glared at his vanishing back. Creatures of habit. The description rankled at the back of her mind for the remainder of the day and the following morning she woke up with a feeling of relief that Ross wasn't going to be around. She was tired of defending Martin to him and to herself. The worst thing was that she couldn't jump right in and wage a heated war in his defence, because that would have been precisely what he wanted, so she had to content herself with being as cool as she could, while inside she felt hopelessly impotent.

At six-thirty precisely next day, Martin arrived for her. She had carried a change of clothes to work and had slipped out of her neat suit into a comfortable pair of jeans, a clinging long-sleeved polo-necked top in pale gold and a loose-fitting tan-coloured jumper with a motto of cream angel fish shot through in a line around it. Martin looked at her appreciatively, while chatting about the outcome of the meeting which, he informed her, he had hurried along so that he could get to her in time.

'You really shouldn't have,' she said, moving to unhook her coat. She turned to smile at him just as the door opened and Ross walked in. She was so taken aback that she paused in mid-air to stare at him.

He was dressed formally, in a white shirt and a black dinner-jacket, with a black bow tie, and an ivory-coloured silk scarf carelessly around his neck. She could see Martin's features freeze with unspoken resentment and she hurried into speech, asking him what he was doing here.

'Have those faxes arrived?' he asked, and she nodded, immediately knowing what he was referring to. He nodded and gave her an insolent, stripping glance, then smiled lazily.

'Have a good time at the movies,' he said, nodding in Martin's direction, the first indication that he had even noticed him, and Martin returned with a tight smile.

'I don't think I like that boss of yours one bit,' he said to Abigail, as they took the elevator down to the ground floor. 'Acts as though he owns the damn world! And I don't care for the way he treats you either.'

'What do you mean?'

They walked out of the building and the cold night air felt like a slap on her face. Martin had his hand at her elbow and she could feel the tension in his body. She could understand it. Ross Anderson could have that effect on people, make them tense and defensive. Seeing them together had been a bit like watching a rabbit next to a jungle predator, and it was no wonder that Martin's reactions were ones of angry discomfort.

'I mean,' he said with exaggerated patience which she found slightly irritating, 'he acts as though he owns you.'

Abigail flushed deeply and did a double-take. 'You're being over-imaginative!' she protested, and he threw her a grim look.

'He acts as though your whole existence is to be at his beck and call. Do you think I didn't notice the way he looked at you when he walked in?'

'Don't be silly,' she said, remembering the cursory flick of those dark eyes on her, making her skin burn.

'He doesn't like me,' Martin said in a tone that bordered on the petulant. 'I could tell at that engagement party. He was polite enough, but underneath it was like talking to a wall of cold, calculating ice. Still, I gave him my opinion on arrogant snobs like him.'

'That's just the way he is,' she murmured soothingly, not caring for this unexpected side to him, and he burst out,

'Don't make excuses for him! The sooner you clear out of there the better, as far as I'm concerned.'

She shoved her hands into the pockets of her coat and felt a sharp twinge of anger.

'There's no point in discussing this,' she muttered.

'I want us to set a date for our wedding,' he persisted stubbornly, 'and I want it to be soon. Within the next six months, then we can start a family and you can tell that boss of yours what he can do with his job.'

He caught her arm and her eyes evaded his.

'Sooner or later, he's going to start trying to turn you against me,' Martin said, with a depth of insight that took her by surprise. 'He strikes me as the sort who would like to run other people's lives for them and that includes yours!'

'You're imagining things. And we're getting in everyone's way.' She began walking and he continued his diatribe. Why, she thought, had Ross Anderson ever gone to that engagement party? Why couldn't he have left well alone?

'I am not imagining things!' Martin erupted. 'He doesn't approve of me for whatever reason and he's going to poison your mind against me.'

He saw the flicker of a shadow cross her face, and said in a so-I'm-right voice, 'Has he said anything at all?'

'No,' she lied feebly, 'not much, anyway. He just thinks that we're creatures of habit. I think he finds that amusing, if anything.'

'I'll bet,' Martin said aggressively.

They had been walking briskly in the cold air towards the Italian restaurant which was only minutes away from the cinema, and he pulled her against him and said huskily, 'Do you think that I'm a creature of habit?' and she looked up into those wide, normally unchallenging, eyes which weren't quite so placid now, with a sigh.

'Is that such a bad thing?' she asked, avoiding the question.

'No,' he conceded grudgingly, 'I suppose not.'

They were regulars at this particular restaurant, and the manager smiled at them as they entered, showing them to the nicest table in the place, in a discreet corner, close to the window yet shielded from casual eyes by a scattering of climbing plants on the window-ledge.

Martin allowed the conversation to drop, but it was still on his mind. She could tell from his distracted manner for the rest of the evening. It was stupid, she wanted to say, to let Ross Anderson influence the way he behaved, but on the other hand she knew that it was stupid of Martin to allow it to. He was nice and reliable and easygoing, but he was essentially weak, and this was something which she was only now beginning to realise. He went with the flow, let himself drift along the currents of life, and avoided anything that promised an uphill struggle. Wasn't that why he had stuck it out in his job for so long? It wasn't invigorating, but it was undemanding, and the option of actually wading his way back into the job market was a task that wasn't, as far as he was concerned, worth the effort.

She had no idea whether this realisation had crept up on her slowly or whether it had advanced in one easy

stride when she was least expecting it, when she had
thought her life to be safely tied up with string, but now
that it had reared its head, it worried away at the back
of her mind, and they parted company, for the first time,
without any of the warmth that they normally did.

She arrived at work the following morning to find that
Ross was late. Unusual for him, and at nine-thirty her
telephone rang. It was Fiona.

'Ross doesn't know I'm calling you,' she breathed
down the line, and Abigail had no difficulty in con-
juring up that feline, white-blonde beauty that could be
as hard as nails or as malleable as putty, depending on
the company, 'but I know what an efficient little thing
you are, so I thought I'd call to let you know that he'll
be a little late this morning. We're at my place
and——' she laughed throatily '—I'm afraid time just
seemed to run away with us. You understand.'

'Of course,' Abigail said stiffly. Why are you telling
me this? she wondered. 'When can I expect Mr
Anderson?' she asked, and Fiona replied with a low,
conspiratorial gurgle,

'Soon, my dear. He's in the bathroom right now. We
had an awfully late night, I'm afraid. It seems to be
something of a habit with us lately. Anyway, please don't
tell him that I called you. He can be terribly dramatic
over the silliest of things. You know men.'

'I'll take your word for it, Miss St Paul.'

'How, incidentally, is that super fiancé of yours?'

'Fine,' Abigail said abruptly, 'thank you.'

'Have you set a date for the wedding as yet?'

'No.' She began doodling on a piece of paper in front
of her, fierce little designs.

'You ought to, you know. Time flies so quickly. One
minute you're over the moon with an engagement, and
the next minute you're looking at five wasted years and

wondering when that little gold band will ever get on your finger!'

'I don't think that would be a problem for me.'

'No,' Fiona agreed, 'he did look desperately keen on you. So absolutely touching.'

Abigail stopped the hectic doodling. Actually, she meant something quite different. She meant that the five years would not really bother her very much, and that thought made her frown heavily. Surely she should be dying to tie the knot? She knew people who had practically booked the church even before they announced their engagements.

'Actually, and this is positively between the two of us——' Fiona's voice was low and hurried and a little embarrassed '—I may soon be in the same position as you! Ross and I, well, I wouldn't be surprised if this man were the one to finally coerce me into marriage. I've had more than my fair share of suitors, my dear, but not tempting enough. Until now.'

Abigail's mouth felt stiff, and she said politely, 'Oh, really? How interesting. Well, I really must get back to work now, if you'll excuse me. Thank you for calling to let me know that Mr Anderson will be in later.'

'Of course.'

There was a click as the receiver was replaced at the other end.

So that was the reason for the telephone call. Never mind an act of courtesy in letting her know that Ross would be late. Fiona had made that phone call to let it be known that Ross had spent the night with her, that, presumably, he spent most nights with her, and that if the wedding bells weren't chiming loud and clear at the moment, then they very soon would be.

Abigail glowered at the word processor and tried to concentrate on what she had to do, but the phone call had thrown her off balance. She stared down at her pile

of work and immediately her mind began to drift along all sorts of stupid, unreasonable lines.

They said that a man in love would very often act out of character. Ross Anderson had never before even thought of sacrificing business for the sake of pleasure, not that she had even known. His work had always come first, and the play afterwards. She had seen him, on occasion, drive himself virtually into the ground, and still have the energy to be in the office the following morning at the crack of dawn.

She had no idea why she was reacting like this. After all, he was entitled to do what he damn well pleased, with whoever, and she decided that it was because if she was forced to alter her view of him, then she might find her respect for him beginning to diminish, and then she would be tempted to look elsewhere for a job. This simple piece of convoluted logic was very appealing, and by the time Ross did make an appearance, she was more or less absorbed in her work.

'Any messages?' he asked, striding into the office with that vitality and dynamism that could still leave her taken aback, and she looked up at him with a blank face.

'Two. I've left them on your desk.'

He divested himself of his jacket and threw her a glance. 'Good. Bit late, I'm afraid, but that meeting with Williams isn't till one, is it?'

'That's right,' she said coolly, and he frowned at her.

'What's the matter?' he asked, stopping by her desk so that she had to look up at him.

'Nothing.'

'Then why do you look as though you're spoiling for a fight?'

'I'm sorry if I gave that impression, Mr Anderson,' she smiled sweetly at him.

'You,' he said, with narrowed eyes, 'are no longer the predictable secretary I had a month ago. I never know

what kind of mood I'm going to find you in when I walk into this office.'

'I do apologise.' She bared her teeth into another sweet smile. That's rich, she thought, coming from you. It's all right for you to be as predictable as a volcano, but if I so much as frown, I'm suddenly responsible for bringing the smooth office machinery to a grinding halt.

He didn't look mollified at her sugary expression. His black brows met and he gave her an impatient, restless look as though he wanted to walk into his office but found that his feet were nailed to the floor by her desk.

'No, you don't,' he snapped. 'Oh, your work is still the same, you make sure that all the letters that I give you get typed and that all the phone calls get made, but you've changed.' His eyes skirted over her briefly, then returned to her face, and when he looked at her it was with narrowed suspicion. 'This isn't some little ploy of yours for getting back at me, is it?'

'Getting back at you for what?' Her surprise was genuine.

He didn't answer. He strolled across to the window by her desk and stared out, then moved across to where she was sitting and leaned right over her, so that when he spoke his breath on her cheek was warm.

'Getting back at me,' he said softly, 'for the remarks I made about that boyfriend of yours being no good for you.'

'No, it is not!' She would have liked to spin around but he had her physically trapped. She couldn't move without finding herself inches away from him, and she knew that that was one thing she didn't want. She clenched her fists helplessly and thought that that would really make his day, to know that something he said casually could have had such an overwhelming effect on

her. Especially, she felt obliged to add for her own benefit, when it wasn't true.

'Sure?' he drawled, with amusement in his voice. 'Your change of attitude looks like a severe case of sour grapes to me.'

She didn't say anything, but her body was rigid with tension.

'Is he your lover?'

The question took her so much by surprise that this time she did turn around, and her mouth went dry.

'That's none of your business.' Her voice didn't sound like hers and she didn't feel as though she belonged to her body at all.

He laughed, and there was something wicked and knowing in his laughter that made her want to hit him.

'That's no answer,' he murmured, and she followed the movement of his mouth with fascination. 'Don't tell me that all that sexy dressing hasn't done anything for your love-life. I've only ever seen you in your bland uniform of suits. Neat and sober. I never guessed that a risqué dress or a pair of tight jeans could alter the image so completely. Don't you turn him on, or is it the other way around?'

'You may find this hard to believe,' she muttered, 'but there's more to a relationship between a man and a woman than sex. You think that desire makes up for a lack of basic friendship, but it doesn't. That's why I could never go out with you.'

'I didn't realise I'd asked.'

She could feel hot colour rush into her face, but it was too late to retract the stupidly spoken words. It wasn't what she had meant to say, not at all. Her brain wasn't working properly, not with him so close to her.

'On the other hand,' he murmured lazily, 'a bit of animal lust helps.' He gave another of those amused

laughs, and she knew that he was going to kiss her even before he did. She could see the intent stamped in those disturbing, gleaming black eyes but she was too frozen to do anything about it.

He lowered his head fractionally, and his lips when they touched hers were explosive. She closed her eyes and half opened her mouth, allowing his tongue to caress hers, while his hand reached up to cradle the back of her neck.

Martin had kissed her, of course he had, but it had been nothing like this. Their kisses had been comforting ones. There was nothing comforting about this. There was hunger in his kiss and it awakened a shameful burning in her that made her whole body feel as though it were on fire. The fire was melting everything inside her, every nerve, every muscle, every pore. Her legs felt shaky and she was glad she was sitting because, if she hadn't been, she would have collapsed.

The demand in his kiss grew stronger, changing from mocking provocation to something more intense, and it galvanised her back into action. She pushed hard against him and he straightened, staring at her, his face unreadable.

They were both breathing heavily, she from mortified embarrassment and shock at what had just taken place between them. He stuck his hands into his pockets, but she was the first to break the silence.

'I'll pretend that that never happened,' she said, trying to be as composed as possible, while everything inside her was still reeling from horror. 'We're both adults, and what took place was a mistake, an error of judgement.' Her eyes shifted away from that hard, masculine face to the shelf behind him, with its row of plants, its *Oxford English Dictionary*, its bright plastic jar of pencils. Those things represented normality.

'Oh, of course,' he said in an odd voice. His lips twisted cynically, and the familiar mocking amusement was back on his face. 'Let's just label it a freak accident and that way neither of us can be held responsible.'

'That's right,' she agreed quickly, not liking his tone.

She thought that he would retort with something biting, some derisive remark on her humiliating rush of desire when only minutes before she had been calmly informing him that desire was nothing compared to friendship. Friendship! He had proved his point and in the most terrible way possible. He had shown her the naked face of passion, because what she had felt just then, for a split-second, was passion such as she had never imagined possible, and she hated him for teaching her that lesson.

How could she ever have thought that Ellis Fitzmerton had taught her anything at all about desire? What she had felt for him had been a shadow in comparison.

Whatever, though, this situation developing between herself and Ross was a dangerous monster. Had she always been attracted to him? she wondered with panic. She had never thought so. She had always thought that his sex-appeal was something that didn't touch her, however blatant it was, that the rapport they felt was founded in their mutual ability to work well together, but maybe she had just been hiding behind closed doors, keeping the monster at bay.

Common sense told her the truth, though. Basically what had applied to Ellis especially applied to Ross. Her mother had always been right. Ordinary girls like her were meant for ordinary men and lived ordinary lives.

Ross was staring at her, not saying anything. He walked away, back into his office, pushing open the door and then slamming it behind him with such force that the room seemed to rattle with the reverberation.

She stared sightlessly at her desk, and thought that what he had just done was like a punch in the stomach. He had taken all her stupid, fanciful notions and turned them on their heads, and in the process had turned her carefully plotted life upside down.

CHAPTER FOUR

ROSS was standing at the office door, his hands in the pockets of his black coat. Abigail noticed him but only out of the corner of her eye. For the past three days she had been doing her utmost not to let him get under her skin, and it was working. Now she made a great show of concentrating on the paperwork on her desk, because she could feel his eyes on her.

'Not leaving yet?' he asked, and she was forced to look at him.

'No, not just now,' she said calmly, 'I've got some more letters to type and I want to clear them before the weekend.' Actually, the letters weren't important, but she didn't want to travel down with him in the lift.

He raised his eyebrows. 'And I thought that women needed hours to get ready for a party.'

This time she gave him her full attention.

'Party? What party? What are you talking about?'

Wrong response. He moved over to her desk and leaned on it, propping himself up by his hands so that his face was only inches away from hers.

'Don't tell me that you've forgotten.'

'What am I supposed to have forgotten?' She was definitely feeling confused now, and he gave her a slow, silky smile.

'The party? The one at the Savoy tonight? Lots of lawyers and bankers? Oh, for God's sake, Abby, I know that you have a lot on your mind with your love-life, but I didn't think that you'd gone completely soft in the head!'

He stared at her and she gasped with nervous dismay. 'Oh, God, the party. The lawyers and bankers one. I'd completely forgotten. I meant to transfer it into my diary but I must have forgotten.'

'Too bad. Now you'll have to rush around because we're due there at seven-thirty and it's nearly six right now.'

'I can't make it.'

'What?' His voice was dangerously soft.

'Can't you get Fiona to take my place?' she asked weakly. She didn't want to go to a party, any party and especially not to a party in the company of Ross Anderson. She had just about made it through the past few days by concentrating hard on her work and besides, she was in no fit mental state to go anywhere. She didn't think that she could manage to act normally when the events of the past few days were still on her mind.

'No, I emphatically cannot get Fiona to take your place. You'll just have to cancel your date.' He straightened and said with a grim smile, 'I'll expect to see you there at seven-thirty.'

Then he was gone and she stood up and began clearing her desk quickly. She was over-reacting, she knew, but Martin's words kept floating back into her head. 'It's that boss of yours, isn't it? That's why you're breaking off the engagement. He's been feeding you doubts, telling you how to run your life. He thinks that, because he can crook his finger at work and you run, he can apply the same principle outside work as well.'

She had denied it vigorously, she had spent a tortuous forty minutes explaining, apologising, squirming at the baleful accusation on his face.

Martin hadn't understood or he hadn't wanted to and, much as she had wanted to spare his feelings, she hadn't told him what had become clear to her ever since Ross had kissed her on impulse, another meaningless action

prompted by curiosity. That however much she liked him, she wasn't in love with him.

Her mother had been shocked, then dismayed, then finally indignant. Heaven only knew how his parents had taken it. She had never had the opportunity to get to know them and it saddened her to know that they would think about her now with parental dislike and resentment.

She managed to make it to the Savoy with only minutes to spare. She knew from experience that this sort of client party did not cater for a lack of punctuality. Drinks would be drunk between seven-thirty and eight, then food eaten between eight-thirty and ten-thirty, then some more drinks which could last until gone midnight. And she also knew that she would have to chat, chat, chat and maintain a bright façade even though she might not feel much like it.

Ross was there by the time she arrived, standing in the midst of a group of dark-suited businessmen. That was another feature of these functions, where other halves were excluded. They were predominantly male. Abigail had never minded. She tended to stand on the sidelines anyway, listening, happy to put faces to the names which she often saw on paper.

He beckoned to her, his eyes flitting over her cursorily, and she accommodated herself into the group, breaking off to chat to the man next to her, whom she had met before and rather liked.

Gradually the group dispersed and he whispered into her ear, 'Very neat. Very serious.'

'What is?' she asked, puzzled.

'Your outfit.'

She went red and he grinned at her with ironic amusement. She had worn one of her old stand-bys, a black suit with an aquamarine silk blouse and a string of pearls.

'I didn't think that the occasion called for anything flamboyant,' she said tartly, and his grin broadened.

'No. You wouldn't want to be responsible for giving anyone here a coronary, would you?'

'I hardly think I could do that,' Abigail said, smiling and sipping from her glass of excellent champagne. She wasn't looking at him. Her eyes were flitting across the crowded room, idly picking out faces that she recognised.

'Oh, I don't know.' His voice was low and lazy. 'You underestimate yourself. You also overestimate some of the old duffers here. Look at old Sir Wilcox——' he inclined slightly so that his voice was a murmur in her ear '—ninety if a day. If he saw you in what you were wearing at that engagement party of yours, he would choke on his gin and tonic.'

There was a sudden thread of electricity between them and she wondered whether she was imagining it. It wasn't the first time that they had been to one of these affairs together and joked good-humouredly about the people there, but never before quite in this vein. She decided to ignore imagination.

'Old Sir Wilcox,' she responded drily, 'is hardly ninety and he happens to be married.'

'Which hardly says anything.'

'Very cynical.' She took another sip of champagne, caught someone's eye across the room and smiled in recognition.

Ross laughed. 'Cynicism is what separates fools from wise men.'

This time Abigail looked at him. 'And I gather you classify yourself as one of the wise men?'

He shrugged and slanted her a sideways look. 'Now it would be very immodest for me to say yes to that question, wouldn't it?'

'And of course, you're nothing if not modest,' she murmured seriously, relaxing as the champagne bubbled

its merry way down her throat and dispelled some of the
anxieties that had been tugging away at her for the past
few days. Wonderful stuff, champagne, she decided.

Two lawyers joined them and they stood there
chatting. Abigail listened while her mind drifted away,
back to Martin.

'Look at all the things we have in common,' he had
argued persuasively. 'We both like the quiet life, we're
neither of us nightclubbers, we enjoy going to the
cinema. We even like the same movies!'

She had frowned, hesitant, confused. Wasn't he right?
Wasn't that love? The pull of attraction, what was that?
Lust, and lust never lasted. It fed, and when its appetite
was sated, it died.

'We're friends, aren't we?' he had asked. 'Well, what
about we see each other as friends? No strings attached.
What would you have to lose?'

So they had parted outside her block of apartments
like the friends Martin had insisted they now were. A
brief peck on the cheek, nothing threatening.

'You're daydreaming,' Ross said into her ear, and she
jumped guiltily.

'I wasn't. I was listening to every word that Gerry and
Robert were saying.'

'Really.' His voice was amused and sceptical. 'I'll give
you the benefit of the doubt, but I want to have a word
with Lord Palfry over there about that takeover that's
in the pipeline, so make sure that the little grey cells are
alert and in full working order.'

Ross could function perfectly well without her, she
knew, but he liked having her there by his side, mentally
taking notes, and this time she listened to every word
that Lord Palfry was saying. The business world was a
complex one. Little snippets of information exchanged
at company affairs such as these had to be filed away
because they could be useful at a later date.

Ross had told her that the very first time she had accompanied him to a client gathering, and she had obediently filed throwaway remarks into the storage area of her brain, amused to find at a later date that he had been right. The strangest things could sometimes have the most meaningful consequences. She could remember, ten months ago, telling Ross lightly that a certain company director was having an affair with his personal assistant, an attractive, bespectacled girl from Arkansas. It had been a flash of insight on her part, a female intuition that stemmed from the way they didn't look at each other, rather than the way they did. Ross had called off a bid to buy the company, and sure enough, a few weeks later, the company director announced his decision to marry his assistant, move to America, and resigned. Shares plummeted and Ross acquired the firm at a fraction of what he would have originally paid for it. Abigail would never have placed that amount of importance on that love-affair but, as Ross had later explained, company shares were a sensitive beast and it sometimes paid to listen to intuition.

Lord Palfry was a wily old fox and an astute financier. When there was a brief pause in the conversation, he turned to her and said, 'Now, my dear, I hope you're doing your duty and filing away everything I'm saying.'

Abigail gave him a startled look.

'I know the way this young lad works,' he said with a hearty chuckle. 'I trained him.'

'A long time ago,' Ross agreed smoothly, with amusement in his voice. 'Lord Palfry lectured occasionally at the university where I studied. He became something of a mentor for me.'

'Tried to get him to come and work at one of my companies, but he refused.' His eyes were bright and shrewd. 'Just as well, in a way. Sharks are difficult to control.' He turned to her. 'How do you manage it?'

'I didn't think I did,' Abigail replied, smiling and he chuckled again.

'That's what my secretary would say, but dammit, I'd be lost if she ever upped and moved on.' He gave a bellow of laughter and gave them a brief nod before edging away.

'Nice man,' Abigail murmured, looking at his departing back, and Ross drained the remainder of his drink and stared at her with one hand in his pocket.

'Don't be deceived by that easy banter. That old dog is as ruthless as they come and I can't see him being kept in line by his secretary, whatever he says.'

'No,' she agreed easily.

'Very few people in this life are indispensable.'

'Of course,' she agreed again, and he frowned at her.

'The problem with women is that they think they sometimes are,' he whispered softly into her ear, and she stiffened.

'Are you referring to me?'

'I am referring to the female species in general.'

'How kind of you to share that thought with me,' she said, and he gave a low laugh.

'Fiona tells me that she happened to mention casually to you that we were serious about one another and you implied that any relationship she and I had could not compare to the relationship you and I have because no one could possibly know me as well as you do.'

Abigail looked at him in stunned surprise but his expression was veiled.

'I never said any such thing,' she muttered.

'Oh, good.' His lips twisted into a smile. 'Because I'm not Lord Palfry and no one controls me.'

'I never said that I did.'

'Not to me at any rate.'

'Nor to your girlfriend.' She could see what Fiona was trying to do: she was trying to drive a wedge between

Ross and herself. For some reason she felt threatened by their working relationship and she was reacting by attacking first and thinking later.

'As a matter of fact,' she said in a honeyed voice, 'I happen to think that you two are very well suited.'

'Oh, do you?'

'Yes, I do.' You're both as manipulative as each other, she added to herself, accepting another glass of champagne from the waitress walking past with a full tray precariously balanced on one palm.

'That must be irksome for you,' he said casually, and she looked straight into his black, assessing eyes.

'What makes you say that?'

'Because you're attracted to me. Aren't you?' He trailed his finger along her spine and her body went rigid with tension. She fought desperately to control the expression on her face.

'I have more sense than to be attracted to you.'

'What has sense got to do with it?' There was an odd look flickering in the depth of his eyes, but he smiled.

'Everything,' she informed him calmly. He had stuck his hand back into his pocket, but her spine still tingled from his touch.

Everyone was beginning to file towards the dining-room. Over one hundred people, all in their sober city suits, faces blending easily into one another, a dark mass with only the odd bright flash of colour from a woman's dress.

They moved to join the crowd, and although her feet were behaving, carrying her along, her head felt hot and feverish.

She realised with some horror that Ross Anderson knew precisely what effect he had on her, and his little speech earlier on had been to warn her not to let her attraction get the better of her sense of judgement. He

must, she thought bitterly, be the most arrogant man on the face of the earth.

She glanced around her and froze. All these people. The chances of spotting Ellis Fitzmerton amid the throng were a million to one. The chances of him spotting her were equally low, but he had. He was staring at her. He had a drink in one hand, and she watched with mounting dismay as he parted a way through the crowd towards her.

It was not really surprising that he was there and she wished desperately that the possibility had crossed her mind earlier, in which case she would have used any excuse in the book to back out.

'Excuse me,' she said to Ross, because the last thing she wanted was for them to meet, and before he could say anything she began walking towards Ellis.

'Well, well, well,' he said, holding out his arms, which she ignored, 'fancy seeing you here, of all places.'

He looked as though he had already consumed a fair amount of alcohol. His eyes had a certain glazed look about them.

'How nice to see you, Ellis,' she lied politely, hoping that Ross had moved on into the dining-room. 'How are you?'

'Good, as always.' The blue eyes lingered over her. 'Hoped you might have returned to the office, paid us all a visit.'

'I've been very busy,' she said, keeping out of reach of his hands. She looked at him critically and wondered what on earth had possessed her to ever be attracted to him. He was good-looking enough, but there was no depth to him. He looked glossy and shiny, like a pretty piece of costume jewellery.

'I'm sure, I'm sure,' he laughed knowingly, and her fists curled into balls.

'And how is Catherine?'

'Pregnant. Married a year ago.'

'Congratulations.'

'You're looking good, Abigail,' he leered, gulping down some of his drink. 'Very good. Edible.'

Abigail cringed back, and he said petulantly, 'No need to act like that. Not as though we don't know one another.' His face cleared, became calculating. 'There was no need to leave because of her, you know,' he said, drinking some more but keeping his eyes fixed on her face. 'We could have carried on what we had.'

'We had nothing.'

'Now, now, it grieves me to hear you say that.' His hand snapped out and his fingers circled her wrist.

'Let me go,' she muttered, tugging.

'I will, but only if you give me a little kiss first.' He smiled coaxingly and she looked at his flushed face with disgust.

'If you don't watch it, Ellis,' she hissed, 'I'll give you a little something else first, and you won't like it.'

He opened his mouth to say something, and a voice said from behind her, 'Let her go. Now.'

They both looked at Ross who was smiling, but it was a dangerous smile, and Ellis's hand dropped to his side.

'Don't believe I know you,' he said and Ross ignored him.

'Come along, Abigail,' Ross said, steering her away, and she didn't know whether she should feel relieved because she had been rescued from an unpleasant situation, or cross because she was a big girl now in no need of being rescued anyway.

Ellis weaved a path behind them.

'Can't believe the amount of people here,' he was saying. 'Surprising really that we managed to see each other.' He had moved alongside them and shot her a look from around Ross.

'Must be Fate,' he said as a joke, and she didn't answer.

'Where's your party?' Ross asked curtly and Ellis blinked at him.

'Over there,' he pointed vaguely, and Ross said in a hard voice,

'Then why don't you remove yourself to them?'

Ellis glared, then said sulkily to no one in particular, 'Oh, fair enough.' He looked at Abigail who by this time was feeling thoroughly embarrassed. 'Off with the old and on with the new, eh, Abby? Don't blame you.' He winked at her and she smiled in frozen humiliation.

He wheeled off in the opposite direction and Ross didn't say a word to her. He released her hand, and they walked to their table in silence.

It was only when they were alone in the taxi and heading to drop her off at her flat, that he said without looking at her, 'Interesting affair, don't you think?'

'The food was good,' she answered non-committally.

'Who was he?' Ross shifted to look at her and she stared back at the shadowed, hard face.

'I used to work for him,' she said. You can never escape your past, she thought. It always catches up with you and at the least expected times.

'Really.'

She could feel his eyes assessing her in the darkness of the taxi, she could hear the wheels of his brain churning over, reaching conclusions.

'Is he the reason you left?' he asked casually. 'At the interview, you told me that you had reached the end of your career prospects at the company you worked for.'

'I had,' Abigail muttered, stubbornly refusing to be led by the nose into a conversation she preferred to avoid. She had spent months keeping herself to herself, maintaining her private life, making sure that Ross Anderson

never ventured too close and now more than ever it was important that she keep him at bay.

'Or maybe you were indulging in an affair that turned sour,' he murmured, and her eyes flashed angrily at him.

'I have no idea what gave you that impression,' she snapped, 'but you're way off target! I left Jacobson and Brown because I was bored and restless. I wanted a change. I needed to work for a bigger organisation!'

'It would make a perverse sort of sense,' he mused thoughtfully. 'You had an unfortunate love-affair with someone unsuitable, hence your rapid engagement on the rebound.'

Abigail felt a wave of humiliating anger wash over her, and she raised her hand to slap him, an impulsive gesture fired by emotion and a need to retaliate.

She hardly saw his hand snap out. She was only aware of it when his fingers bit into her wrist. He yanked her hand down, pulling her forward towards him.

'Too close to the truth for comfort, Abby?' he whispered.

'You have no right to speculate on my personal life.'

'Why does it matter so much to you?'

'Because...'

'Because you're accustomed to being secretive? Hiding yourself away from prying eyes? Taking refuge in that shell of yours the minute you think someone is getting too close?'

'No!' She hated him for doing this to her, for making her heart beat faster, for making her feel this awful, compelling attraction when she, of all people, should know better. Ellis had been right about one thing. Seeing him like that, out of the blue, had been the hand of Fate, showing her the living proof of her own past mistake, pointing out that mistakes were there to be learnt from.

'You've got to face your shortcomings,' her mother had always told her, 'you're not beautiful, so don't expect things to fall into you lap. Work hard and you might get somewhere but don't expect people to trip over themselves offering you things on a silver platter.'

'How close has this boyfriend of yours got to you? Do you keep him at a distance as well?' he pressed, and she didn't answer. If she didn't say anything, then she reasoned there was a limit to how far he could needle her. He would have to give up in the face of silence.

'No comment?' he asked, with a short laugh.

'That's right.'

'Why? Because it's none of my business?'

'That's right.'

'You're so damned uptight.'

She ground her teeth together and he laughed, raking his fingers through his thick, dark hair.

'You'll get high blood-pressure, bottling everything up inside you like that. You ought to take a look at your face!'

'I know you think it's a great game, but it's not funny.' She could feel tears pricking the back of her eyelids and she blinked rapidly.

'You've had a repressed life.'

'Stop trying to analyse me!' And then she did the unthinkable. She burst into tears. She couldn't seem to help herself.

Ross drew in a sharp breath and put his arms around her, cradling her against him, stroking her hair, and she burrowed against his shoulder. It felt good to have his arms around her.

'Don't cry, Abby,' he murmured. He produced a handkerchief and she wiped her face.

'I'm fine.' Her voice sounded choked. 'I'm all right. I don't know what came over me just then.' She tried

to pull back from him, and he released her but only to tilt her tear-stained face upwards.

'I apologise if I upset you,' he said roughly, his voice awkward. She had never heard him apologise to anyone before and it was clear from the expression on his face that the instinct was alien to him.

'You didn't,' she muttered, dabbing her eyes and wishing that the taxi driver would stop lingering over the route back and put his foot on the accelerator.

He looked down at her and then inclined his head to brush his lips against her cheek. It seemed almost accidental when his mouth found hers and began gently exploring it, tracing the outline of her lips with his tongue, tasting her with leisurely thoroughness. Instinct was telling her something, but she couldn't quite hear it over the roar in her ears.

She reached up and linked her fingers behind his black head, and her breasts pushed against his chest. His hand curled into her hair and she gasped as his other hand moved to cup her breast, kneading it gently. The sensation was agonisingly exquisite.

The fever which had started in the pit of her stomach now spread outwards until she felt as if she were burning up all over. He unbuttoned her jacket and continued caressing her through the fine material of her aquamarine blouse. Her nipple was aching, and his finger found the hard nub and he began rubbing it, playing with it through the lacy bra, making comforting noises.

She squirmed against him, breathing thickly, and he unbuttoned her shirt and scooped his hand down inside the bra so that her breast nestled into the palm of his hand.

Was there ever an experience as erotic as this? His black eyes never left her face, even though his breathing was as uneven as hers and there was no longer anything at all soothing about his actions now. There was an

urgent demand there, matching hers, making her head spin.

When the taxi pulled up outside her house, neither of them was aware of it until the driver coughed discreetly but firmly from the front seat. The practised cough of someone who had seen it all before, and Abigail jerked away from Ross and began buttoning her blouse, her jacket, her coat with unsteady fingers, not looking at him.

There was nothing to be said. She wished that she could blame *something*, but she couldn't. The effects of the champagne had worn off long ago and face it, she told herself with scathing disgust, you didn't exactly scream with outraged horror when he began comforting you.

'Abigail...' he muttered, impatiently reading her expression of mute hostility.

'Don't say a word. Just don't.'

His lips thinned, but she was beyond caring. She snatched up her evening bag and pulled open the car door and the freezing air wafted in, another sharp dose of reality.

She turned to him and said distantly, 'I'll be in at the usual time tomorrow morning. I don't expect I shall see you first thing; you've got two meetings lined up.'

He looked back at her, his eyes hooded, then he shrugged and drawled indolently, 'In that case, I shall see you after lunch. I'm expecting two calls from Bob Reingate and the marketing director. Could you fix meetings for me with them the week after next?'

'Yes.' There was a silence, then he nodded briefly, dismissing her, and she slammed shut the taxi door.

Pity, she thought, two hours later when she still couldn't get to sleep and had been over what had happened between them in such detail that she was going

crazy. I was a sobbing wreck and he took pity on me. First an object of curiosity, now an object of pity.

She would pretend that nothing had happened because what other option was there? But she couldn't pretend to herself. She was violently, stupidly attracted to him and the only halfway good thing about the whole situation was that that attraction had been controllable.

Last night, she thought, as she prepared for work the following morning, was the culmination of a week of worry. He was there, a sympathetic shoulder, but now she realised that if she couldn't control her responses to him, then she would have to leave.

She worked swiftly and silently through until three o'clock, skipping lunch, and feeling that now familiar lurch inside her when the office door was pushed open and Ross strode in, pausing to stand by her desk.

'You've been busy,' he said, looking at the stack of letters neatly piled on her desk, and she smiled.

'They need your signature.'

'In that case . . .' He perched on her desk and took his fountain pen out of his pocket. She watched his dark, bent head as he flicked through the letters, signing them.

When he raised his eyes to hers, she was proud of herself for her outward appearance of calm.

He knew that she was attracted to him, but she was also going to make sure that he knew, just as clearly, that she was not about to have an affair with him.

'Where's your engagement ring?' he asked abruptly, and she frowned.

'Forgot it by the sink in the kitchen,' she lied swiftly, acknowledging that the pretence of still being engaged was no bad thing.

'I don't believe you.'

'I'm not asking you to.'

He shrugged and smiled drily.

'You're damned stubborn, Abigail Palmer,' he said.

'Yes, I am.'

'Is it your way of telling me that last night never happened?'

She flushed but didn't look away. 'How did your meetings go?'

There was an odd tenderness in his eyes, but he said easily, 'Fine.' He stood up and adjusted his tie absent-mindedly. 'Profits are going to go way beyond target, at least for the first six months.'

'Congratulations.'

'A good time for investment,' he said, 'which is why I shall be flying to Boston in a couple of days' time. Have you got a passport?'

'Yes, why?' Then the impact of what he had asked hit her between the eyes.

'Because you're coming with me. I'll give you details and you can book the flights. First class.'

'No,' she said instinctively, because even in the space of one second she could see all the problems posed by being continually in his presence for days on end, and not liking any of them. 'I mean, surely you need me here...'

'If I did, I wouldn't have asked you to come along,' he replied with irrefutable logic.

'Martin and I...' she persisted, mentally rummaging around for any excuse, and his expression went a shade cooler.

'Cancel whatever has been arranged. I'm not asking you to come, Abigail——' he leant towards her '—I'm telling. If you value your job, you'll unearth your passport and pack your bags in time for tomorrow.'

'How long will we be there?' she asked with a sigh of angry defeat.

'Three nights.' He began walking towards his office. 'Book us at the Boston Harbour Hotel.'

'Planes *could* just be full,' she informed him with an edge in her voice. 'Hotels *could* just be booked up.'

'I don't think so.' He shot her a lazy smile over his shoulder. 'Not if you use my name.'

It was only when she later replaced the receiver of the phone, when the airline and the hotel proved as accommodating as he had predicted, once his name was mentioned, that the dreadful uneasiness which she had felt the minute he had issued his command began to sink in.

The thought of being with him in Boston filled her with dread. She knew all about being sensible, she could write a book on the subject, but she had already seen how weak good sense became when faced with that *frisson* of sexual excitement that both lured and terrified at the same time.

In her neat, ordered life, everything had suddenly gone haywire. Boston, she knew, was not the place to try piecing things together again.

CHAPTER FIVE

Ross was resting in the seat next to her, his eyes closed. She looked at him out of the corner of her eye, aware that at any minute he might suddenly open his eyes, with the alertness of a cat, and she didn't want him to catch her staring at him. But he fascinated her. He had, she acknowledged, always fascinated her, right from the very beginning, but that sort of stolen fascination was only a seed. It needed the elements to nurture it, to make it grow, and she had always made sure that those elements were never allowed to get a foothold. She worked hard, head bent, eyes down, aware of his love-life but making no comment on it, and making damn sure that her personal life stayed right out of the picture. But things had changed. The overall picture was the same, she still arrived for work and did her job, but the emphasis had shifted. Now her personal life seemed to swamp her all the time, and Ross Anderson invaded her thoughts like weed that had taken root and in so doing had begun a steady takeover.

She reverted her attention to the screen in front of her. The in-flight movie was a thriller which seemed to have remarkably few thrills and a disproportionate amount of violence, but her mind continued on its one-way track, analysing emotions which she would have preferred to keep buried.

Martin had been casual enough about her sudden departure to Boston and she had been relieved about that, but also a little saddened. She could already feel them drifting away from one another, and even though part

81

of her wanted that, there was another part that felt
alarmed and scared that a relationship which, at least
on paper, had been so promising could end with such
apparent ease. What did that say about her ability to
fall in love with a man who could provide her with the
emotional security she wanted?

'You'll live to regret it,' her mother had said, the voice
of doom as always. 'You would have had a good, solid
life with Martin.'

'Perhaps I don't want good and solid,' she had ventured, and she could almost hear her mother puffing in
irritation down the telephone.

'Fine,' her mother had said. 'Well, you just go right
ahead searching for adventure and, mark my words,
you'll end up with egg on your face. I don't want to
remind you of the state you were in when that business
with your *last* boss came to an untimely end!'

'I wasn't in a state,' she had pointed out reasonably.
'A little upset, maybe, but hardly in a state.'

Her mother could be downright objectionable at times,
although she had a point. Martin *would* have been a
very stable, reliable husband, and high adventure *was* a
risk she was not prepared to take.

She stared at the screen. Now there appeared to be
some kind of frantic car chase taking place which involved quite a lot of guns and screeching of wheels.

She would have to watch herself with Ross. She had
never had to before because she had always suspected
that when he looked at her he saw an efficient piece of
office machinery, but now he knew that she was attracted to him and that made her vulnerable.

Physically Ross Anderson was a sexy man, a powerful
man who was as ruthless as he was charismatic. Men
like that might as well have had 'Danger' stamped on
their foreheads in bright neon lettering, as far as she
was concerned.

She was absently thinking, letting her mind drift along where it wanted, when she felt her headphones being lightly pulled off her head and she turned to see Ross looking at her with sardonic amusement.

'What are you doing?' she asked, startled.

'You're not paying a blind bit of notice to what's going on up there,' he said, dropping the headphones into the pocket of the seat in front of him. He sat back and clasped his hands on his lap, his head tilted at an angle so that he could look at her.

'Of course I was!' she protested immediately, because not paying a blind bit of notice to the movie was infinitely preferable to feeling the rush of nervous tension that his dark eyes induced in her.

'Well, then, tell me what it was about.'

'Two prisoners,' she said succinctly, 'a daring escape, a few car chases and several policemen looking earnest but baffled.'

'So something intellectual, in other words.' He gave her a warm, relaxed smile and she smiled back at him drily.

'In other words.'

'Not your cup of tea?'

'Not really,' she admitted. 'I prefer something a bit more soothing on the nervous system.'

She lay back, offering her profile to him, her eyes closed.

'Like *The Sound of Music* perhaps?'

'Don't knock it! I saw that five times when I was young!' Ross could be very friendly, she thought drowsily, when he wasn't being provocative or else bellowing orders out at her.

'And I haven't seen it once,' he said ruefully. 'Was I missing anything?'

'You'd have hated it. It's very sentimental and a little on the sloppy side.'

'How do you know I would have hated that? I can be very sentimental when the situation demands.'

'I'll bet,' Abigail muttered drily and he laughed.

'Now who's guilty of making sweeping generalisations?'

She opened her eyes to look at him. 'I just can't imagine you being sentimental,' she mused. 'It's a bit like trying to imagine primitive man being sentimental with a club in one hand and a dead boar in the other.'

'I don't think I could lift a dead boar single-handed.' His eyes swept over her face, vaguely unsettling her. 'I see that the engagement ring is still conspicuous by its absence.'

'I beg your pardon?' The question caught her by surprise and she sat up, frowning at this turn in the conversation.

'I'm surprised you haven't got around to retrieving it from the kitchen sink.'

'All right.' She sighed. 'If you must know, we've decided to call off the engagement. There. Satisfied?'

'The question is, are you?'

She looked across at him and maintained a façade of calm self-assurance.

'Of course I'm not satisfied,' she retorted. 'Of course I'm not happy that my relationship with Martin has ended. He was—is—an extremely nice man.'

'But niceness wasn't invigorating enough for you.'

He phrased that as a statement rather than a question and she could feel herself getting angry at the unspoken satisfaction in his voice that she had merely done what he had recommended in the first place. No doubt he was also thinking that the reason behind it was the fact that she was attracted to him, and that made her even angrier.

'We're still good friends,' she said through gritted teeth, and he gave a hoot of laughter.

'Friends! The concept of a man and a woman being good friends without some element of sex involved is beyond me.'

'Well,' Abigail said coldly, 'it would be, wouldn't it?'

'Meaning?' he asked, but his voice was still amused.

'I feel sorry for any man who only sees women as conquests.'

'You're misinterpreting what I'm saying.' He was still smiling. 'It's perfectly possible for a man and a woman to be the best of friends, but not without at least an awareness of sex. They might mutually choose not to act on that awareness, but it would still be there.' His voice was husky. 'Wouldn't it, Abby?'

She heard the timbre of his voice with a jolt of alarm.

'If you say so,' she agreed with a shrug. 'You're the expert.'

He frowned at the lack of response. 'Well, I'm glad that you came to your senses.'

He relaxed back in the seat and there was a smile playing on his lips.

'So am I.' She paused, then carried on without inflection in her voice. 'Although, unlike you, I don't believe that the world revolves around sex. If it did, what hope would there be for anyone having a successful marriage?'

His eyes flickered across to her. 'And a successful marriage is what you're after?'

'Of course it is. What woman isn't?' She gave him a blank smile. 'I'm sure that Fiona is as eager to get married, for instance.'

'Really.' The smile had left his face now and she was glad.

'She more or less told me so herself.' She gave him a surprised glance. 'Weren't you aware of that?'

'Stop trying to be clever.'

'I'm so sorry.' She smiled again. He didn't mind provoking her into awkward situations so that he could sit back and smile at his handiwork, but he disliked being at the receiving end of the same game. 'Isn't marriage on your agenda?' she asked sweetly.

'You are beginning to irritate me,' he said with a heavy frown, and she manufactured a contrite expression which met with an even blacker expression.

'I'm so sorry.'

'And stop apologising,' he muttered, 'that's beginning to get on my nerves as well.'

'Your nerves do seem to be a bit delicate at the moment,' she said, concerned. 'I can't imagine why.'

'Oh, go back into your shell,' he told her, 'you're easier to handle that way.'

That made her laugh and it forced an unwilling grin out of him. Their eyes met and she looked away quickly because in that split instant something strong and silent hummed between them.

'OK. In that case, may I have my headphones back, please?'

'Go right ahead.'

She bit back a sigh of frustration. He wasn't going to reach them for her, and he knew as well as she did that for her to reach them herself would mean her leaning across him, practically lying across his lap.

'You're not enjoying the movie anyway,' he said, when she made no move to get them, 'you told me that yourself. You were having a far better time playing with me.'

'No, I wasn't,' she said, going red.

'No?' he murmured lazily, flashing her a sideways smile that had a hint of challenge in it. 'You seemed to be thoroughly enjoying yourself just then, trying to provoke me into a reaction. How could we have spent

months working together without me realising that you have claws?'

'I have not got claws!' He was back in control now.

'Point proved.' He closed his eyes and yawned and she glared at him from under cover.

Shortly afterwards, the plane began to descend and the confused turmoil of thoughts running through her head was submerged beneath the general fuss of buckling the seatbelts and stretching slightly to steal glances through the window.

She didn't see much, of course. They were landing in darkness and there was nothing to distinguish the twinkling lights of Logan airport from any other airport in any other metropolis.

A chauffeured car was waiting for them once they had cleared Customs. It was a relief not to have to stand in a queue for a taxi, especially as it was cold, much colder than it had been in London, with the sort of dry feel that made you long to have every exposed part of your body under wraps.

She had reserved one of the penthouse suites for Ross and something altogether less imposing for herself three floors down. Seeing the hotel now, she didn't doubt that her less imposing room would be marvellous and the mind boggled to think what the penthouse suite would be like.

'Dinner?' he asked, turning to her after they had been checked in. 'There's a restaurant here, as well as a bar, and the food in both is very good.'

She shook her head, shying away from the thought of having dinner with him. 'I'm very tired. Exhausted, in fact. I'm going to retire to bed and order room service.'

He shrugged, not bothered by her refusal.

'In that case, I'll expect you to join me for breakfast. Eight sharp. I want to go over some things with you before the first meeting.'

She nodded. It was an immense relief to be back in her safe secretarial role. The bellowing, she had decided on the plane, was infinitely better than the amused, probing curiosity.

She had no idea just how tired she was until she had had her bath and her dinner, which had arrived promptly. A salmon salad with avocado, lots of brown bread which was the best she could remember tasting, potato crisps and a bottle of ice-cold mineral water. She sat on the bed with her book optimistically in front of her, and after fifteen minutes she was fast asleep.

The following day, she was glad that she had had a good night's sleep. There was a series of meetings to attend, complex affairs during which she took notes and listened first-hand to Ross's dynamism as he discussed high finance with board directors, bankers, and lawyers. He had a sharp mind and an ability to read the flow of currents, so that every problem thrown at him was met with an answer. He wanted a takeover of an American firm, one that was ailing but wary of being ruthlessly poached.

Over dinner, which was hosted by one of the lawyers, they discussed legal details of the takeover, while she watched and listened, mesmerised by Ross's breadth of knowledge. Occasionally, when the conversation turned to lighter matters, she contributed something, but she was content to remain in silence.

At the end of two long days and two gourmet dinners which were merely a continuation of business, but over a four-course meal, she wistfully thought that she had managed to see precisely nothing of Boston, so it was with a certain amount of excitement that on her last day she was told to relax and sightsee.

'But won't you need me at the meetings with Don Huston and his partner?' she queried over breakfast, and Ross shook his head.

'It's all but sewn up,' he said, with the confidence of the tiger that had just accomplished a difficult kill. 'The nuts and bolts are all in place. My lawyers in England can take over the rest when we get back.'

'Does it give you a thrill to do something like that?' Abigail asked curiously.

He sat back and looked at her, and she didn't need him to answer to work out what his reply would be. It was written on his face. He enjoyed the cut and thrust of power, the wielding of his intellect.

'I wouldn't do it if it didn't,' he said coolly. He took a sip of coffee. 'What about you? Did you enjoy it?'

'Very much,' she admitted, 'though I couldn't see myself doing the same thing. I wouldn't have the heart for it, never mind the brains.'

He looked as if he were about to say something, but then he glanced at his watch and stood up.

'Shame we can't sightsee together,' he murmured, watching her, and she smiled politely.

'Better that only one of us freezes to death out there rather than both of us!'

'Get used to it,' he said, slipping on his jacket. 'I spoke to someone in England last night and it's bitter over there. They predict snow.'

'Weathermen always get it wrong though, don't they?' She was smiling, but the smile was laboured. Could the 'someone' he spoke to have been Fiona, by any chance? Had he been missing her?

It was easy to forget that Fiona existed, that life back there in London, in the real world, existed. Boston, for all its hard work and business dinners listening to legal talk, was like a step out of time. She had forgotten all about Martin and the headache that she had left behind, and the thought of Fiona, back there, enjoying her nightly conversations with Ross, was a sharp blast of reality.

She spent the remainder of the day enjoying the city as much as she could, given the weather. Whenever it became too unbearable outdoors, she found warm sanctuary in one of the malls and nursed her hands around a cup of coffee. No plans had been made for that evening, though Ross had hinted that he would be visiting a friend and she would be free to do what she liked. What she liked, at the end of what turned out to be a very long but highly enjoyable day, was another stab at room service. The first time had been so fantastic that she wanted to give it a second try.

She arrived back at the hotel at five-thirty, had a very leisurely bath, washed her hair, which she bundled up into a turban, and then dialled for delivery of smoked chicken with all the trimmings.

When she heard the knock on the door half an hour later, she trailed across to the door, still inappropriately clad in her white towelling bath robe, with her hair now combed but damp around her face, and opened it, smiling.

The last person she expected to see standing there was Ross. Her eyes opened and she automatically took a step backwards. He was dressed casually, in a pair of black trousers with a black jumper. With his dark colouring and hard features, there was something distinctly menacing about him. Was this what a highwayman looked like? She supposed so.

'What are you doing here?' she asked, clutching the lapels of her bathrobe as if they had a will of their own and were threatening to flap open at any moment.

His eyes drifted over her, taking in the tightly clutched bath robe, and his lips curled with amusement.

'Not what you're obviously afraid of,' he said, leaning against the door-frame. He wasn't barging into the room, in fact he wasn't making any effort to enter at all, but she still found his presence oppressive.

'Do you think I'm about to rape you?' he asked, his eyes gleaming. 'Or do you normally answer the door with an expression of panic on your face?'

'I wasn't expecting you,' Abigail said stiffly. 'I've ordered some room service and I was expecting one of the hotel staff.'

'Ah. So you would have been quite relaxed, dressed like that, in front of a complete stranger. What does that say about me, I wonder?'

She knew very well what he was hinting at. That he made her nervous, and the logical step from that would be why.

'I thought you said that you were going out this evening. To see a friend.'

'Did I?' He looked at her blandly, enjoying her discomfort as much as she was hating it. The man was a sadist.

Behind him, a tall, thin teenager arrived with a trolley of food and Ross stepped aside to let him enter. As Abigail ushered him in, thanked him, gave him a tip, she was acutely and agonisingly aware of Ross still standing there, watching the proceedings with leisurely interest, making no move to go.

'Well,' she said, once the boy had exited, red-faced, 'have a good evening. I shall see you at breakfast.'

She made as if to close the door and he reached out lazily with one hand and forced it back.

'You're coming out to dinner with me,' he decided coolly.

'Thank you,' she said equally coolly, 'I'd kill for that, but as you can see...' She spread her arm in an expansive gesture to include the neatly arranged food, now on the low coffee-table in the middle of the room. She gave him a rueful smile which he ignored, stepping into the room, his hands in his pockets, looking around him with absent-minded curiosity.

'Leave it,' he said. 'And get dressed. The table is booked for seven-thirty. Seafood, I thought.'

'I told you,' she repeated crossly, 'I'm not coming out to dinner with you. I've made alternative arrangements. Thank you all the same.'

It was water off a duck's back. He continued prowling around the room, before moving to stand in front of her.

'I don't feel inclined to indulge in a pointless debate about this,' he informed her with enough boredom in his voice to make the blood rush angrily to her head. 'We both know that you're coming with me, so why waste time arguing the toss?'

There were quite a few retorts that flew to mind at that high-handed, arrogant observation, but she found that when she opened her mouth nothing emerged but a strangled, fairly inarticulate sound.

He smiled. 'Good. Now off you go to change. Nothing too formal. Legal Seafoods is a casual sort of place.'

It was futile protesting further. He would, she knew, remain where he was until she gave in, and being dressed in a bath robe with her hair hanging around her face in wet tendrils was not an advantageous point from which to conduct a winning argument.

Two months ago, she thought, Ross Anderson would never have been able to rouse this level of emotive response in her at a dinner invitation. Two months ago, she would have accompanied him politely to dinner, they would have discussed work, exchanged pleasantries on the weather, the city, whatever. Two months ago she still had her head firmly screwed on.

She bad-temperedly headed towards the bathroom, changed into a simple long-sleeved dress in a shade of dusky blue, applied some make-up, slipped on a pair of grey, high-heeled shoes and then reluctantly faced him across the bedroom.

'There,' he said, looking at her, 'that wasn't the end of the world, was it?'

He knows that phony placatory tone gets under my skin, she thought, but she wasn't going to let him see that, so she smiled, shrugged and fetched her thick grey cardigan from the wardrobe, as well as her coat.

They travelled down to Reception in silence and Ross made sure that a taxi was ready and waiting for them directly outside the hotel before they braved the freezing cold.

'Not a good idea to scour the streets in search of transport,' he murmured, allowing her to slip into the back seat, then lowering his long body in beside her.

'Must be awful having to wait around for public transport,' Abigail agreed easily. She could sit here and comfortably discuss the weather till the cows came home, she thought.

'A place like this caters for the cold, though,' he explained. 'A lot more happens under cover. You could survive the winter months living like a mole.'

'I don't think I like the thought of that,' she said, staring through the window.

'You could get used to it,' Ross said drily, and she felt his eyes on her averted face. 'One could get used to anything, even if one doesn't necessarily like it.'

Was he trying to tell her something? She glanced at him sharply, but in the semi-darkness of the taxi, his expression was bland, unreadable.

'It's the basic human instinct for survival,' she said neutrally, not dwelling on unspoken innuendo, which was probably just a figment of her imagination anyway.

They travelled the remainder of the distance in companionable silence, and over an excellent meal of Cajun-style fish and home fries they discussed everything, from the business transaction which Ross had successfully

completed to places in Boston which he had seen during past visits, but which she had had no time to discover.

And of course, they drank. Superb white wine. After two glasses, she was feeling pleasantly relaxed. Those intense, glittering dark eyes no longer sent her into mild panic.

It was ten-thirty by the time they made it back to the hotel, and as the lift doors opened to her floor she turned to him with a smile and thanked him for an enjoyable evening.

He stepped out of the lift and she felt a tiny shiver of alarm as he followed her to the bedroom door, watching as she inserted her card into the lock and pushed open the door.

'Invite me in for a nightcap, Abby,' he said with a slow smile.

'We have to be up early tomorrow,' she answered in what sounded a very feeble protest to her ears.

'So we have,' he agreed, entering the room, and moving to sit on the small two-seater sofa by the window.

She looked at him out of the corner of her eye, torn between common sense which told her that Ross Anderson, sitting there on the sofa, casually relaxed with his fingers linked behind his head, was a dangerous man, and a strange excitement that terrified her.

She handed him his drink, a whisky and soda, and took a sip from hers, looking at him over the rim of her glass.

'Talk to me,' he commanded. 'Don't just stand there acting as though I've suddenly turned into the big bad wolf.'

'What would you like to talk about?'

'How about the latest movie you've been to?' He swallowed his drink and cradled the empty glass in one hand. 'Or the kind of music you like. No, dammit!' He stood up and walked across to her, towering over her.

'No, tell me why you became a secretary, not that you're not a damn good one, instead of going to university. I listened to you over dinner, talking about the business deal I made over here. Everything sank in, didn't it? You understood the lot, right down to the legal jargon which most people would have switched off from early in the proceedings. So with a brain like that, what are you doing working for me?'

'I could always hand in my resignation,' Abigail quipped, and he frowned darkly and impatiently at her.

'You're avoiding my question.'

'All right,' she muttered awkwardly, wishing that he would return to the sofa so that her breathing could get back to normal. 'I left school at sixteen because it never occurred to me that I was bright enough to continue my studies.' Her head snapped up and her mouth was set in a stubborn, defensive line, as though he had criticised her, even though he hadn't uttered a word. 'Well, it's all right for you! You had parental support, you were always——' her voice faltered, and she looked down at her hands, wrapped round the glass like a vice '—encouraged, no doubt. But with me, with me it was different. My mother never expected me to aspire beyond what she saw as the acceptable course for a girl like me, from a working-class background.'

'And you listened to her?'

'Of course!' She shrugged her shoulders, and attempted a light smile which met with a hard, questioning stare that made her feel slightly giddy. 'My mother longed for a son. I was a disappointment to her. Nothing I ever said or did ever seemed to be good enough. I guess by the age of sixteen the constant silent battle had worn me out. Don't get me wrong,' she said quietly, 'I love my mother, and now I understand her better. She had a hard life bringing me up. It was a struggle. She may not have expressed it properly, but

deep down all she wanted for me was a life of comparative safety, a stable job...'

'A reliable husband.'

'Yes! Is that so wrong?'

Their eyes clashed and she heard the heavy thud of her heart, felt the dryness of her mouth.

'Understandable, but still a waste of talent.' He bent his head and brushed her lips with his mouth. He reached for her glass, which he placed on the sideboard, without his eyes leaving her face.

She might have had two and a half glasses of wine, and she certainly felt unsteady, but she wasn't so unsteady that she didn't realise the sudden danger she was in. Ross Anderson was a powerful man who played games by his own private set of rules.

His hand curled into her hair, pulling her head backwards, and she opened her mouth to protest. Nothing emerged. His mouth found hers and the sweetness of his tongue against hers scattered her unvoiced protest. She closed her eyes and wrapped her arms around his head, groaning huskily as his lips trailed over her skin, over her neck, a leisurely, intimate caress that made her gasp.

He lifted her off her feet in one easy movement, and placed her on the wide double bed, with his arms still around her. In the still room she could hear her rapid breathing echoing his, urgent, feverish sounds that seemed to be coming from another person altogether, not her, not careful Abigail Palmer.

His hand moved along her back, slowly unzipping her dress, slowly unclasping her lacy bra, and an immense yearning invaded her body. She moaned and felt as though she was burning up as he eased one arm out of the dress, then the bra, exposing her breast with its hard, aching nipple.

With an instinct born of desire she cradled the full swell of her breast, offering it to him, and he took the

nipple into his mouth and sucked hard on it while his
tongue flicked hungrily over the sensitised tip.

He pressed her flat against the bed and continued to
kiss her mouth while he completed the manoeuvre of
slipping her dress down to her waist and removing her
bra, then, with trembling fingers, she undid the small
buttons of his shirt and circled his broad torso with her
hands.

This was madness, she thought, but something inside
her, stronger than reason, wanted the madness to continue. He caressed both breasts with his hands, massaging them, licking the milky whiteness, teasingly taking
his time before he began to nuzzle the large brown
nipples. It was an eroticism which she had never experienced in her life before.

She had always thought that lovemaking was something gentle, a soft, easy meeting of bodies. She had
never imagined for a moment that it could be like this,
like being set ablaze, with every pore and nerve on fire.

It was only when she felt his hand along her thigh,
cupping the moistness between her legs, that the enormity
of what she was doing really sank in, and it sank in with
dizzying speed. One minute she had been lost in a crazy
world of sensation and the next she was staring at the
horror of a situation which had gone completely out of
hand. Her eyes flew open and she jerked back with a
stifled gasp of dismay.

He lifted his head, but she was already pulling back,
desperate to put some distance between them. She
wriggled against him, frantically yanking up her dress.
It didn't take him long to figure out what was going on.
Anger darkened his face and that made her move even
faster, leaping off the bed and watching him, ridicu-
lously, as if any moment he would attack.

CHAPTER SIX

THEY stared at each other for a long time in the dimly lit room, then he stood up, looking at her with derision as she flinched back.

He hadn't got undressed. Only the front of his shirt was undone and she made very sure that she didn't look at the sliver of brown chest exposed. She had just about given up on relying on her brain to have any input into what her body wanted to do.

He began doing up the buttons of his shirt, then he slipped the black jumper over his head and stuck his hands in his pockets. They were still looking at each other like two warring animals. He was the first to break the silence.

'I can't stand women who play games,' he said derisively.

'What are you talking about?'

'You know damn well what I'm talking about.' There was hostile aggression underneath the cold voice. 'Does it give you a kick to lead a man up the garden path and then, once he gets to the top, inform him that the front door is locked and bolted? Was that the score between you and your boyfriend? I thought that you had seen him for what he was, but maybe I was wrong.' He took a step towards her and her nervous system went into overdrive. 'Maybe,' he said silkily, unsmiling, 'he saw you for what you really were. Is that closer to the mark? Did he get fed up with kisses on the cheek and promises of better things to come?'

'I said I was sorry...'

He took another step towards her and she tried to edge a little further away without actually running. Cool and controlled was good, running like a frightened rabbit was not.

Very easily, Abigail realised with rising panic, this could degenerate into something more than simply unpleasant. Ross Anderson was a tough man who went for the kill and he was accustomed to having his way with women much more sophisticated than she was. There was no point in flinging counter-accusations at him, or even in holding her hands up in horror at what had happened. And there certainly was no point in apologising further. He looked as though if she uttered another sorry he would throttle her.

She would have to be composed and she would have to try and defuse the situation. Later, alone, would be the time for angry debate with herself.

'Look,' she said quietly, ignoring the curl of his lips, 'I'm very sorry things got out of hand.'

'So you keep informing me.'

'Do you *have to loom*?' she snapped. 'You're making me very nervous!' Stay calm, she told herself, and took a few deep breaths. 'There's no point in discussing this. I'm sorry...'

'If you say that once more,' Ross warned her, enunciating every syllable very carefully, 'I will personally see to it that you have something to be sorry about.'

'Am I supposed to be quaking with fear at that?' she flung at him angrily, throwing composure to the four winds. 'Because if that's what you're aiming at, then you're way off course. A woman has every right to say no!'

He moved swiftly. One minute he was standing at a reasonable distance away, close but not too close for comfort, and the next minute he was towering over her, his black brows drawn together in rage and she dis-

covered that breathing was not a function to be taken for granted. She was having a great deal of difficulty with it. She was also beginning to regret her spark of retaliation.

He circled her, as if looking at something distasteful. 'I feel sorry for that boyfriend of yours. He'd have needed a sledgehammer to break through to you.'

That stung, and she didn't say anything. In a protective gesture, she folded her arms around her breasts and lowered her head.

'That's nasty,' she mumbled finally, and he raked his fingers frustratedly through his hair.

'Oh, what do you expect?' he muttered harshly. 'Every time I come near you, you freeze.'

'You shouldn't be coming near me at all!' Abigail flung at him. 'You have a girlfriend! Have you forgotten? You never used to... It was never like this... We worked well together!'

She knew what she wanted to say and she knew that she was being inarticulate, but he understood because some of that tightly controlled rage began to dissipate.

'Fiona and I are not married. I have no hold over her and she has none over me. If I were interested in that sort of possessive relationship, I would be married.'

That was not the impression Fiona had given her, Abigail thought, but this was neither the time nor the place to have a debate on the subject. In fact, there was no time or place when the subject could be conceivably discussed because it was none of her business and he was telling her as much with his tone of voice.

'As for things being different between us——' his mouth twisted '—they just are. Don't ask me why, but they are.'

The air trembled between them. She was so aware of him that she was finding it difficult to think.

'Perhaps you're right,' she said in a low voice, 'but whatever impression I gave, I do not want to jump into bed with you, or anyone else for that matter, because the chemistry is right at the time. That's not for me.'

'Are you afraid of sex?' The question hung in the air and she didn't know where to look. She knew, without doubt, that she would never be so mortified in her entire life. From thinking that she was a tease, which was bad enough, he now thought that she was a freak with deep-rooted psychological problems.

'I think I need to sit down,' was all she said, and she didn't wait for him to answer. She went across to the bed on legs that felt like pieces of wood, and sat down heavily.

'I'll understand if you no longer want me to work for you,' she ventured into the silence.

'Wouldn't that be an easy way out for you?' he said coolly. 'If you don't have to confront me on a daily basis, if you don't have to face the fact that you're attracted to me, then you could pretend that it was all some kind of aberration. Because that's what you want, isn't it? You don't want to be confronted with anything that threatens to shake that aloof demeanour of yours.'

'I don't want to discuss this.'

He ignored that. 'Life isn't about avoiding strong emotions. And you still haven't answered my question.'

'Look, I'm not the sort who can make love to a man because my hormones are egging me on. I might be tempted, but in the end the temptation wouldn't be worth the regret.' She looked at him. 'I know you probably wouldn't understand, but that's just how it is.'

He sighed and there was more impatience there than fury. The anger had abated.

'You're building castles in the sky,' he said, his voice rough. 'Over the years you've had it instilled in you that

safety is the most important thing, but safety is dull, uninspiring.'

'And danger isn't for me.'

'Not danger, excitement.'

'I've had danger,' she said bitterly, without thinking, 'I've had damned excitement, and it was an experience I won't ever repeat!'

'Ah.' He sat down next to her on the bed, and eventually she said in a stiff little voice,

'And what does ah mean?'

Looking at him wasn't a good idea, she decided, so she didn't. But she couldn't avoid seeing his hands, lightly clasped on his lap, with their dark fine hair and their graceful, powerful lines.

Every nerve in her body felt stretched with unbearable tension.

'That man...'

'Yes,' she said rapidly, 'that man.' Suddenly her legs wanted to move and she stood up, hugging her arms around her, and paced across to the window to look down. Outside was the harbour, a dark black mass at this time of night.

He was waiting for her to carry on, and she did, in a voice that barely rose above a whisper.

'You were right when you said that I left my last job because of an affair.' She glanced at him with wary, antagonistic eyes. 'Yes, I had an affair with Ellis Fitzmerton. I must have been out of my mind. We had been working closely for some time and one thing just seemed to lead to another.' She gave him a defiant look but he remained silent. 'I had never before done anything like that; in fact I had never before been attracted to a man like that.'

'A man like what?'

'He was charming, self-confident.' She hesitated and thought that there were other, more appropriate adjec-

tives she could find now to apply to him, but at the time she had been dazzled by the superficial. She had spent a lifetime being reminded of her limitations and Ellis had reached out and offered another glimpse of herself. The glimpse he had offered had looked bright and clever and attractive and it was only when reality had taken over that she had had the painful duty of seeing herself for what she was.

'Empty,' Ross said with an edge of acid scorn in his voice, and her head snapped up to look at him.

'Yes, empty! I can see that now, but I was vulnerable then.'

'And you're not now?' he enquired softly.

'I'm not stupid. I was burnt once. I don't intend to stray close to the fire again.'

'So you got engaged to the first man who represented the opposite of that disaster of a man you got involved with.'

'No!'

'Yes!' He stood up and walked towards her and she held her ground. 'Admit it, you never loved Martin Redman. He was an alternative that presented itself when you needed it.'

'He is a very nice man.'

That had a familiar ring to it, she knew that she had defended him before in those same words, but Ross was staring at her, his mouth set, forcing admissions on to her.

'You can't judge the rest of the human race from one bad experience,' he said, and that made her smile wryly.

'No? Is that an order?' She looked right into his eyes and felt a stabbing shiver of forbidden desire. It was almost a pleasure to fight it back. 'I may not be a mental giant, but I'm not dimwitted enough not to realise that only a fool goes through life lurching from one experience to another, without learning lessons along the

way.' She looked at him steadily and when she spoke
there was a hardness in her voice, 'In other words, Mr
Anderson, you may be an attractive man, but I am not
going to sleep with you. You are not about to become
mistake number two on my list of regrettable incidents.'

'You can't let the past control you, Abby,' he said
softly, 'and you can't escape from feeling, however much
you'd like to.' He reached out with one hand and stroked
her arm, then the curve of her neck, then the soft swell
of her breast.

'I think it would be better if you left now,' she said
quietly. It was a tremendous effort to get the words out
because her throat seemed to have seized up, but he had
to go. That was all there was to it.

'Because you're afraid of me?'

'Because I'm afraid that, if you don't, I shall be forced
to hand in my resignation immediately.'

'You don't mean that.'

'Watch me.'

His hand dropped and he said with low emphasis, 'I
am not Ellis Fitzmerton.'

'No you're not,' Abigail agreed, 'you're probably far
more unscrupulous.'

His lips tightened and she felt a flare of sudden
triumph. He was nothing like Ellis Fitzmerton, she knew.
Ellis had been self-serving and, in the end, cruel. He had
laughed at her and her silly delusions, and Ross would
never do that, but in the end she still stood to be desperately hurt by him if she made the mistake of giving
in to temptation.

Cards were on the table, and as far as she was concerned she didn't want him around. He saw too much
and she didn't care for the way he could read her feelings.
The last thing she wanted was for him to read the guilty
craving in her, the awful part of her that kept telling her
how much she would have enjoyed the brand of ex-

citement that Ross Anderson had been willing to offer, never mind lessons from the past, never mind the tight-lipped admonishments from her mother which had followed her through the years.

'You use women,' she said, relentlessly carrying on because it was better to be hung for a sheep than a lamb. 'You might tell yourself that you play fair with them and that you're both aware of what you're doing, but in the end you use them. I don't know if curiosity about me changed things between us, but whatever it was, I don't intend to be used.'

The contours of his face hardened. 'No, you don't intend to be hurt, Abby, except that when you think about it there's no sure guarantee that you won't be, in whatever relationship you find yourself in. You might find yourself getting involved with a man who's up for a damned sainthood, but that still doesn't mean that you might not end up being hurt. Do you think that you can control your life to that extent?' There was mockery in his voice and in his eyes.

'I could try.'

'And what kind of life would that be? You might just as well never leave your flat in case one day you get run over by a bus. Life's a gamble.'

'But there are some gambles I'm not prepared to take. You're quite right, I might step out into the road one day and get run over by a bus, but on the other hand there's more chance of that happening if the road is teeming with buses and I'm crossing it blindfold.'

He shrugged coldly and she could tell that he wasn't about to prolong the conversation. A vague expression of boredom smoothed over the taut lines of his face.

'Fine. I get your point. We need to leave here by eight-thirty at the latest,' he said, turning away. He walked across to the door, then said over his shoulder, 'I'll meet

you at Reception promptly.' Then he was gone, and the silence in the room echoed around her.

She removed her clothes, then had a shower. A long shower. She wanted to wash away all that shameful lust that had consumed her earlier. She would have washed away her thoughts if she could.

The temptation to hand in her notice the minute she got back to England was very strong indeed. He had been spot-on when he had told her that she was terrified of having to face him on a daily basis. He had also been spot-on when he had said that that was the coward's way out. If she left the company, she would be running away, and in the end running away didn't solve anything. You could flee to the ends of the earth, but your thoughts and feelings went with you and you would never be able to shift them.

Also, she thought with brutal honesty, she would never find another job like the one she had. For a start, the financial package which she was on was superb. Ross Anderson paid well, well enough for his employees to be reluctant to leave, but, more than that, he had gradually allowed her to take more and more initiative in her job and where else would she be able to find employment as satisfying?

She climbed into bed, but it was hours before she managed to fall asleep, and she awoke the following morning heavy-eyed and still tired.

There was no time for breakfast, so she telephoned for coffee and fresh bread to be sent up to her room, and she ate on the move, packing and dressing in between mouthfuls of bread and coffee.

He was waiting for her in the foyer when she arrived, casually dressed in grey trousers, thick ivory-coloured jumper, and his black coat.

Immediately she felt her stomach begin to go into knots, but when she finally approached him he was polite

and distant, ushering her out to the limousine which had been ordered by the hotel.

Nothing had happened. The night before had been relegated to history. This was what his attitude told her and in a way she was greatly relieved.

The flight over seemed to take far less time than the flight across, and he worked through much of it, dictating letters to her, which she scribbled down in her folder.

The deal which he had just accomplished was going to involve quite a few changes in England. People would have to be transferred, at least temporarily, to America. Confidential information was discussed and the wrenching anxiety which she had felt the evening before began to ease away.

They landed seven hours later to bitter cold. There had been a light fall of snow in their absence and most of it still clung to the roofs of houses and unused cars.

'I suggest,' he said, once they were in their taxi, 'that you take the rest of the day off work, and probably tomorrow as well.'

'I don't feel tired,' Abigail said promptly, and he gave her a wry look.

'It'll hit you, believe me.'

'Will you be going in to the office?' she asked with curiosity, and he nodded.

'What about the letters?'

'I'll get Angie to do them.'

'No.' She shook her head slowly. 'I'll come in this afternoon, type them up so that they're ready to go in the evening post. I know they're important.' She glanced at him and tried not to betray the shiver of awareness that rippled through her. 'But,' she said, hitting on an idea which had only just occurred to her out of the blue, 'if you don't mind, I'd like to take a few days off work.

I've still got quite a bit of holiday quota left from last summer.'

He looked at her, then said without emphasis, 'Of course. Where do you intend to go?'

Polite question, but she knew what he was thinking and he was right. She needed to get away, she needed somewhere isolated where she could think without the interruptions of her daily life.

'Just to the Lake District. My friend's parents have a little cottage up there and she's always told me that I could use it any time I wanted, and I never have.'

Emily, in fact, another childhood friend with whom she had remained close over the years, despite the physical distance between them and the contrasting life-styles, had had the cottage in mind as some kind of lovers' haven. She lived in Wales with her husband and three children and had spent years trying to convince her friend that marriage was the only desirable course in life. She, Abigail and Alice had been a close-knit threesome for as long as she could remember and Emily, by far the most matronly of the three, had always seen it as her mission in life to settle them down. It irritated Alice and amused Abigail.

'I know the Lake District quite well,' Ross said blandly; 'my uncle has a house there. Whereabouts is your friend's cottage?'

Abigail told him and he recognised the area instantly. He chatted to her about it, with one eye on the time, and Abigail half listened while she mentally pictured what his uncle's house looked like. A stately mansion, no doubt, as far removed from her friend's cottage as Windsor Castle was from her one-bedroomed apartment. That only reinforced her own stupidity in allowing him to get as close to her as he had the night before. They were from different worlds, they breathed different air. She slid her eyes along to his face and watched him

through lowered eyelashes, watched the firm curve of his jaw, the sensual moulding of his mouth, the dark, mesmeric eyes. Was it any wonder that he had not expected her to pull back when he had begun his advance? He hadn't known about Ellis then.

She thought of the feel of his body under her fingers and the sensation was so immediate that she had to look away from him hurriedly.

Yes, she thought, she really needed some time to think. She had already broken off her engagement, but that had only put a part of her life back into perspective. There was another bit which was still full of shadowy misgivings, and she needed space and isolation to deal with those.

The taxi dropped her off first at her flat, where she quickly showered and changed into some clean clothes, then headed off to the office. As Ross had said, tiredness and jet-lag began to creep in as soon as she set foot in her flat. By the time she made it to the office she couldn't wait to type her letters and then hurry back home to sleep.

She had expected to find Ross there, but he didn't appear and she jealously wondered whether he had been sidetracked by more exciting prospects, namely Fiona, who must have been waiting with bated breath for him to return from America.

She decided that she didn't care one way or another, and concentrated on working as quickly and efficiently as she could.

As soon as the batch of letters were in their envelopes, she grabbed her coat and headed for the lift. She had taken a taxi to the office because she had been in a hurry to get there, but she caught her usual bus back to her flat and arrived exhausted forty-five minutes later. The traffic had been slow to stop much of the way, and the weather outside was becoming colder if anything. People

flew over the pavements, clutching their coats to stop
them from billowing in the wind, their faces, illumi-
nated by the street-lights, pinched and tight lipped.

The first person she called, as soon as she got into the
apartment and had divested herself of her coat, was
Emily, who happily agreed to lend her the cottage, giving
her careful instructions as to where to find the key, which
was under a mat in the log shed at the back, and which
had always been kept there because of unexpected visitors. In return, she indulged in fifteen minutes of gleeful
curiosity, only cutting it short when two of the three
children became too unruly to be ignored.

'Are you sure that married life with children is as
tempting as you've always led me to believe?' Abigail
teased. 'It just sounds very noisy to me.'

'Give it time,' Emily promised darkly. 'You too will
join the ranks of the blissful when you finally tie the
knot.' As yet she didn't know that Martin was no longer
in the picture, and Abigail omitted to mention it because
she knew that that would have led to at least another
twenty minutes of remonstration and sympathy, genuine
enough, never mind the decibels of the screaming
children.

The second call she made was to Martin. She didn't
know why but it was almost as though she needed to
hear his unthreatening voice to shift her thoughts back
into focus. Besides, she had promised to phone him on
her return; he had reminded her that they were, after
all, still friends.

When he finally answered the telephone he sounded
cheery and vaguely guilty, and it was only when she
questioned him that he let slip, bit by gradual bit, that
actually he had been seeing something of Alice in her
absence.

Well, he protested when she greeted this piece of reluctantly volunteered information with surprise, she *had*

been the one to break off their engagement, hadn't she? And Alice had been very sympathetic. And she *had* more or less made it perfectly clear to him that there was no point in pursuing their relationship. Her attitude had been, as far as he could read it, that he suddenly wasn't quite good enough for her.

He hadn't given her a chance to dispute any of these points, which he enumerated as though he had rehearsed them in advance. By the end of his monologue, the sheepishness had more or less vanished, replaced by accusation. I'm seeing Alice, his tone implied, and basically this is *all your fault*.

You're a free man, she told him, you can do as you please, and there's no need to find excuses, but by the end of the conversation she was feeling foolishly upset.

They said that women were unpredictable, but men were not nearly the straightforward creatures that women were led to assume. Martin had found solace with someone else with a rapidity that left her breathless, and Alice, in all honesty, was far more his cup of tea than she, Abigail, was. But he could hardly have been deeply in love with *her* if he had replaced her in a matter of days, could he?

She had to remind herself that he was a free man and if he had found comfort with Alice, then why should she begrudge him that? She had to tell herself that it was better for him to move on than to stand still, hoping for their relationship to get back off the ground. Nevertheless, she doubted that she would ever see Alice in the same uncomplicated light.

She slept heavily that night, and awoke early the following morning to a sky that was leaden grey. Overnight the temperature had dropped still further, but she didn't care very much. She would be safely cocooned in a train, then in a rented car which she had arranged to meet her

at the station, so she would not be obliged to face the
fierce cold for any length of time.

She was about to leave when the telephone rang. It
was Ross. She heard the deep timbre of his voice with
muted panic.

'You can't go to the Lakes,' he told her, without both-
ering to go through the preliminaries of Hello, or How
are you? or even Thanks for the letters.

'The train leaves in thirty minutes,' she informed him
by way of answer, 'I was just on my way out.'

'They expect severe snow there by tomorrow evening.
You'll be snowed in.'

And unable to return to work, she thought with
cynicism. Was that the reason behind the warning? That
she might find herself trapped for a few days and go
over her allotted leave? There was a high-powered
meeting scheduled for the day after she was due to arrive
back in London. He would be furious if she was unable
to attend. He had become accustomed to the way she
worked, and because of that they functioned well
together. He depended on her being able to make notes
of the important issues, ignoring the dross which clung
to most business meetings like useless seaweed. There
was, she reflected, a ruthless streak in Ross that would
have stunned her if she hadn't become so accustomed
to it over the months that she had worked for him.

'I'll make sure that the cottage is well stocked,' she
said. She had packed a few things, and would have time,
just, to make it to the corner shop for a few more.

'This isn't a laughing matter,' Ross said grimly down
the line. 'If the snow is anywhere as bad as they predict,
then you could find yourself stuck up there for more
than a few days.'

'Thanks for the warning,' Abigail said, 'but I really
must be on my way now or I'll miss the train. I'll see
you when I get back, Mr Anderson.' She replaced the

receiver and felt a vicarious thrill at having been the first
to end a conversation between them. She could imagine
him cursing softly under his breath, and half pitied the
next human being to walk through the office door.

She wasn't unduly worried by the prospect of snow.
In fact, she rather liked the thought of it. It would be
comforting to be cocooned in a cosy little cottage while
the weather outside ranted and raged. Emily had told
her that the place was always well supplied with food,
because it was heavily used, and the log shed would be
stocked to the ceiling with logs. She doubted that there
was any basis for Ross's fears that she would be snowed
in indefinitely. She had never actually been to the Lake
District, but this was England, after all, not Iceland,
and snowstorms tended to be short lived.

The train left exactly on time and she spent the journey
staring out of the window at the passing scenery and
reading her book. It was relaxing. All her worries seemed
to diminish in direct proportion to the amount of distance between herself and London. She wondered idly
whether she would forget them completely if she vanished out of England altogether and found a job in some
remote part of the world. Doing something wildly different like teaching English to the Eskimos. Or was
English their native tongue? The question amused her
until she felt herself getting tired, and the next time she
opened her eyes was when the train jerked to a stop at
her station.

Train, she mused, on time, car, she found, awaiting
her at the station, as duly promised by the rental
company, sky, she noticed, not looking ominous. Life,
she decided, definitely taking a turn for the better. She
hadn't thought of Martin once, and Ross—well, she had
managed to keep his image resolutely to the background
and every time it had threatened to intrude on her well-
being she diverted her thoughts to something else.

The cottage, admittedly, took some time getting to and she was exhausted by the time she finally arrived, driving very slowly because it was pitch black. Also, she didn't like night driving. She was unaccustomed to driving at all, because she had no car in London, where it would have been more of a liability than an asset, and when she did borrow her mother's car, most of her driving was done during the day.

For the first time she wondered what she would do if it started to snow, and the prospect of that, miles away from civilisation, didn't seem quite so adventurous as it had done several hours earlier in the busy warmth of the train.

The cottage, she found, was small, but exceedingly comfortable, with the sort of homely atmosphere of a second home that was very well used and maintained.

Emily had told her that it was on regular loan to any number of friends who fancied a weekend away, and during the summer months it was as busy as any hotel.

'All spongers,' she had laughed, 'ought to be charged rent, but most of them have been taking advantage for so long that they would collapse on the spot if money was suggested.'

They all, she had said, paid by way of leaving some present behind, and, as Abigail browsed through, it wasn't difficult to find the presents. Several boxes of biscuits and chocolates, an extremely well stocked supply of drink and lots of little ornaments which differed wildly in taste.

Ranged along the fireplace were dainty porcelain figurines which nudged alongside garish, souvenir ceramic ornaments, and an assortment of umbrellas stood in a massive colourful pot, clearly forgotten by their owners.

The furniture, a three-piece suite, was worn but pleasant and the faded floral pattern was just right for the place. It lent it a warm glow.

She sank into the nearest chair and closed her eyes, relishing the peace and quiet. She could never retire to the countryside, she had lived too long in a city to find solitude appealing, but sitting here she could understand the allure.

There had been no need to light the fire because there was central heating, which she had switched on as soon as she had arrived, but tomorrow, she thought, tomorrow she would be highly industrious and get the logs going.

Over the next two days, life drifted into an easy, comfortable pattern of breakfast, followed by a walk, then lunch, much reading and not too much thinking, and in the evening she lit the fire and after supper was content to simply lie on the sofa with her feet up and set her mind to the strenuous task of dozing and reading.

Three more days of this, she thought, and she would return to London fortified against anything. Fortified, particularly, against her silly preoccupation with Ross, which, in the solitude of a cottage miles away from anything, now appeared laughable and a little crazy.

Abigail stuck her book on her stomach and grimaced. Silly, she told herself. Silly and crazy.

She closed her eyes, fell asleep, and woke up the following morning with a stiff neck and a back that felt as though it had been twisted into several contradictory directions.

Automatically she went across to the window, yawning and flexing her arms, and then stopped.

No snow, no indication of it at all since she had arrived. She had blithely assumed that the forecasters, as usual, had been up to their old tricks of exaggeration.

Outside the sky was a heavy, leaden colour and light flakes were drifting down, nothing too terrible but not exactly heart-warming either.

She had a quick breakfast of cereal, and then changed into her jeans, with several layers of clothes over them and her waterproof coat.

Outside the sudden drop in temperature was noticeable. She stuck her hands into her pockets and within minutes of walking she could feel her face beginning to go numb with cold. I am, she laughed out loud, Scott of the Antarctic.

She knew not the first thing about meteorology but she peered up at the sky anyway, and dubiously decided that things didn't look too bad. It must have started snowing only shortly before she woke up with the stiff neck and the dodgy back, because there was no build-up on the ground. That was good news. Less good was the fact that, although the fall was slight, it was persistent, and it was cold enough to ensure that what fell stayed.

She spent another half-hour walking, and then made her way back to the cottage.

She tried her routine of lazily doing nothing much, but she couldn't manage it because by three o'clock, with darkness already beginning to throw its mantle over the ground, she was now worriedly assessing the situation and feeling no humorous comparison to Scott of the Antarctic whatsoever.

Her original conclusion that things didn't seem too bad was starting to wear thin at the edges. The snow was getting thicker. It wasn't so thick that you couldn't see between the flakes, but it was whirring down steadily and the branches of the trees were already white and covered.

She had an early supper, at six, and drew the curtains. No point gazing out and contemplating the worst, was there? She had earlier made sure that the supply of logs by the fire was restocked from the shed at the back, and the cupboards, thank heavens, had enough food to feed

the starving thousands for quite some time. Visitors had generously supplied grateful leaving gifts of tins of salmon, pâté, tuna, in additional to the usual dried foods.

She had never actually been snowed in, anywhere, in her entire life. It had always been the sort of thing that she had read about in books, something that sounded exciting and vaguely romantic.

She had a bath, then changed into her pyjamas and drifted back down into the small sitting-room, curling into one corner of the sofa and resisting the temptation to do a spot check on the weather.

It was a bit of a shame that there was no telephone in the place. Emily had said that her parents had never thought it right to have one installed, just as there was no television set. They had liked to have that total feeling of getting away from it all.

With snow outside, Abigail wryly thought that a link to the outside world, however pointless, would have been welcome. Right now she felt a bit like the last remaining survivor on planet Earth.

It was terribly comfortable in the sitting-room. With the log fire burning, she felt warm and cosy. She could quite happily drift off, but the memory of the aches and pains which had accompanied her last lapse the night before were too vivid in her mind for that mistake to recur.

When she felt her eyelids beginning to droop, she went upstairs and promptly fell asleep.

She didn't know whether it was the need to go to the bathroom that awakened her, or else the deep cold that had managed to wriggle under the blankets and clamp itself over her body. She shivered and reached to switch on the bedside light and felt a sudden, stiffening jolt of panic when nothing happened. No warm glow, nothing.

She threw back the blankets, sprang out of the bed and tried the switch by the door. Nothing.

Oh, God, she thought, don't tell me the electricity's gone. No electricity equalled no lights, equalled no heating, apart from the fire in the sitting-room.

She fumbled her way down the stairs with her arms clasped around her, thankful that she had at least had the sense to pack her warmest pyjamas, and hopelessly tried the remaining light switches, even though she knew that she would find the same irritating, unrewarding click.

The log fire had died, and after what seemed like hours rooting around in the dark while her eyes acclimatised to the blackness, she managed to get it going again.

Then she sat down in front of it with her feet tucked under her and thought.

Snowed in and freezing wasn't a winning combination. Her mind threw up a lot of very graphic images of what could happen and none of them was very pleasant.

What if, for instance, the logs ran out and she couldn't make her way to the shed because she couldn't get out of the house? What if the matches ran out and there were no more packs in the house? She hadn't thought to look when she had first arrived because there were sufficient on the mantelpiece and besides, there was always the central heating, but without matches or heating she would freeze to death.

She laughed uneasily to herself. Her imagination was running away with her, for heaven's sake. This was England. The electricity would be back within hours, most probably, and the snow wouldn't stay on the ground for longer than a day, a couple at the outside. In the morning she would have a good laugh at herself.

Her head began to droop down, and with some effort she made herself go back up to the bathroom, this time

with some light from the fire to guide her. She would
hunt down some candles when she got back downstairs.
Everyone had candles in their house. Even *she* had
candles in her little apartment, even though the electricity had never yet failed her.

But she didn't get around to it because when she returned downstairs, the first thing she did was to peer
outside, and that was when she saw something moving.
Out of the corner of her eye. The glimpse of a shadow
which was gone even before it had had time to register
on her consciousness.

Then she began to feel real terror.

CHAPTER SEVEN

ABIGAIL didn't know what to do. The easiest thing would have been to tell herself that she had imagined it all, but the sickening feeling in the pit of her stomach was telling her too strongly that that was no figment of her imagination. She had really seen something, and it hadn't been some harmless animal seeking shelter.

She thought quickly. The door at the back was bolted, a precaution that came as second nature to her from living in London where unlocked doors were open invitations to burglars.

The front door was likewise bolted. That just left the windows which, for a man determined to enter, would provide very little by way of a barrier. All he would have to do would be to break the glass and open the window from the inside, and he wouldn't even have to watch how much noise he made because he could make as much as he liked without fear of being heard by anyone.

She tiptoed across to the window, cautiously drew back the curtain but only fractionally because she had no intention of drawing attention to her presence in the cottage, and looked outside, but everything was silent. The snow, climbing steadily up the trunks of the trees, was still falling and there was a stillness about the scene that now struck her as very eerie indeed.

She frowned, wondering what to do, whether there was any useful weapon in the house apart from one of the logs by the fireside which would be too unwieldy to be of any use, when there was an almighty bang on the door and she jumped in shock.

Then there was another bang, and she nervously made her way to the front door and looked at it as if searching for inspiration.

The man, seven foot two in her imagination and bearing a strong resemblance to pictures of primitive caveman, was going to enter. He would either assume that no one was in if she didn't answer, and then break in, or else, if she did answer, would immediately realise that she was alone and vulnerable and would break in. Either way he wasn't going to leave politely the way he came.

'Yes!' In the quiet of the room, her voice bounced off the walls and startled her with its volume. 'What do you want? My husband is asleep upstairs and I shall call him immediately if you don't go away at once!' By the way, she wanted to add, he's a bodybuilder with a black belt in karate and can break bricks with his bare hand. 'If you're looking for shelter,' she shouted, hoping the caveman wouldn't sense that she was scared stiff, 'use the log shed. You'll be out of the snow.'

'You damned woman!' An answering voice roared back at her, slightly distorted through the thickness of the wooden door. 'Open this door right now, or I'm bloody going to freeze to death out here!'

'That's it!' she yelled back. 'I'm going to fetch my husband this instant!'

'You don't have a husband!'

He had been spying on her. Watching her. How else did he know that she was on her own? The thought of the caveman looking at her while she took her walks, peering into the cottage as she cooked her dinner and read her book, sent a chill through her.

'You open this door now, Abigail Palmer, or I'll throttle you the minute I get my hands on you!'

The relief that washed over her was immense, and she fumbled with the bolt on the door, letting in a gust of

freezing wind and snow, and also Ross Anderson, dressed in black from head to foot and not looking very happy.

'What are you doing here?' she stuttered, her eyes wide, her mouth half open with delayed surprise.

He didn't answer. He slammed the door behind him and then strode across to the fire where he took off his gloves, flung them on the nearest chair, and began warming his hands, rubbing them together to get the blood circulation going again.

Abigail watched him with a stunned expression and finally he turned to face her.

'You took your bloody time opening that door,' was all he said, and she glared at him with resentment, forgetting how terrified she had been less than fifteen minutes earlier.

She had been having a fine time, she fumed, snow or no snow, electricity or no electricity, and now her peace had been invaded by the last person in the world she had any desire to see. To top it all, he was already acting as though she should be grateful to him for turning up here in the dead of night and scaring her half to death!

He removed his coat, which joined the gloves on the chair, then raked his fingers through his hair.

'That feels better,' he said. 'Would you like to get me a cup of coffee?'

She remained where she was and folded her arms with a look of purpose on her face.

'Would you like to tell me what brings you here?' He might be her boss, but if he thought that she was going to run around behind him in her free time, fetching cups of coffee, then he was in for a sad shock. She was here to relax, and the sooner he took himself off, the better.

He slumped on the sofa and rubbed his eyes with his thumbs, and reluctantly she went into the kitchen with the matches and made them both some coffee, while she continued to seethe inwardly.

How did he find her? The question answered itself almost immediately. She had asked her where she would be staying, because he'd said that he knew the Lakes very well, and she had told him, in some detail, where the cottage was. She had never expected the piece of information to have brought him to the doorstep.

She went back out into the sitting-room, handed him the coffee, which he took without looking at her, and then she sat down on the ground with her back to the fire.

'I haven't heard you rushing to thank me,' he said, when he had first drained the cup.

'Haven't you?' she said in a lemony voice, a mixture of sweetness and acidity. 'Well, thank you so much for giving me the fright of my life. It really made my day.'

'Wrong answer,' he drawled, and this time his eyes fell on her for the first time. They wandered over her, in her pyjama-clad state, and she was deeply grateful that the only light in the room was the shadowy light from the fire. That way he wouldn't be able to make out the red embarrassment on her face.

Now that he had removed his coat, she could see that he was wearing a deep-coloured jumper, grey or black, she couldn't tell, and a pair of dark jeans. His shoes he had kicked off but he was still wearing his socks, which were the same dark colour as the rest of his clothes.

'You still haven't told me what you're doing here,' she pointed out, flicking her hair behind her small ears, and he watched every movement in detail.

'I would have thought that it was self-explanatory.'

'I must be a bit dense in that case, because I'm stuck for an explanation.' She sounded controlled enough, but she didn't feel controlled. In fact, she wasn't going anywhere near him if she could help it. She had deluded herself into thinking that Ross Anderson had only been part of the reason for her decision to flee London for a

few days. Now, with him lying there on the sofa with his feet crossed at the ankles and looking, infuriatingly, as though he damn well belonged there, she realised that he had been the whole reason for her sudden departure.

She had always acknowledged his staggering, terrifying sexy charm, the sensuality beneath the dark, hard features, but it was only recently that she had acknowledged the effect that they had on her.

Physical attraction seemed too mild a term for the overwhelming, choking craving that she felt for him, and it was that that had sent her running up to the cottage so that she could muster her forces and return to London with her personality intact.

'I came,' he said lazily, with his eyes closed and his hands linked behind his head, 'because I heard on the television that snow had started here and was due to worsen, and that some parts had already lost electricity. I knew where you were and I telephoned the weather centre for more information.'

'How did you make it here?' she asked.

'Oh, I didn't drive the distance from London, before you overwhelm me with your concern. I took a helicopter to my parents' house and made it to within striking distance of this place in the Range Rover, but then the roads seized up on me and I had to walk the rest of the way.'

'How far?' she asked, horrified.

'About a mile.'

'Thank you,' she mumbled under her breath, and he said, opening his eyes,

'I don't think I caught that.'

'Thank you,' she repeated in a loud voice, 'but there was really no need. I was fine.' Scared witless but fine. Now I'm anything but fine.

'I take it the electricity's been cut off.'

'Yes,' she conceded, 'some time during the night. I woke up to go to the bathroom and nothing. So then I came down here and lit a fire. Why didn't you knock on the door,' she asked suspiciously, 'instead of lurking around the cottage?'

'Because,' he said patiently, 'I didn't know whether you were asleep or not. I knew the fire was lit, but you could have done that and gone back upstairs to bed, in which case, if the back door had been unlocked, I would have simply let myself in without waking you.'

He stood up abruptly and stripped off his jumper to the short-sleeved T-shirt underneath, then she watched in horror while he divested himself of his trousers and socks, and lay back down on the sofa clad in only the T-shirt and a pair of boxer shorts.

This wasn't going to do, she thought worriedly, this wasn't going to do at all. Her nerves were all over the place and her heart was doing a frantic tattoo in her chest.

'Damp,' he explained casually, yawning, and rather than just sit where she was, frozen and staring, Abigail stood up and busied herself laying the clothes in front of the fire. With any luck they would be bone-dry within minutes and he could get them back on again.

His eyes were on her, she could feel them sending prickles of awareness along her spine.

'While you're on you feet,' he said, yawning again, 'you couldn't get me something to eat, could you?' It was phrased as a question, but he didn't expect her to refuse.

'It's late. Have you any idea what time it is? You can't be hungry.'

'Try telling that to my stomach.' He studied her face and, with a shrug, she headed back towards the kitchen, and groped through the drawers until she found some candles. Then she lit three of them and stood them up

in a line on the window-ledge. Making two mugs of coffee by the light of the fire in the sitting-room was one thing, but fixing a meal was another.

He should never have come, she thought to herself disgruntedly. Did he make a habit of showing up unexpectedly where he wasn't wanted? He might have thought at the time that he was doing the right thing, saving her from a fate of hypothermia, but that didn't alter the fact that he was here now, larger than life, making her feel jittery and on edge.

She opened a can of baked beans, which had been in the cupboard, buttered a couple of slices of bread, which she had thankfully brought with her in some abundance, and covered the lot with grated cheese, then she reluctantly walked back into the sitting-room and handed it to him.

'It'll have to do,' she informed him, and he shot her a dry look.

'I wasn't expecting caviar and lobster.' He began eating, and she returned to her safe place by the fire, with her arms wrapped round her knees.

'How long do they expect the snow to last?' she asked after a while, and he replied, concentrating on the plate of food,

'A few days.'

'A few days! A few days! That's ridiculous!' We can't stay cooped up here together for a few days, she wanted to wail. I'll go to pieces.

'Have a look outside,' he returned calmly. 'I'll bet you that it's gathered force even since I've been here.'

She walked across to the window and looked out, and he was right. It was snowing furiously and the snow was catching on absolutely everything and sticking there. In the morning, the place would look like a picture postcard, but not one in which she particularly wanted to feature.

'Point proved?' he asked in a voice that told her that he was only too aware that his presence in the cottage was filling her with misgivings. He deposited the empty plate on the ground and she eyed it with her hands on her hips.

'Fine,' she said. 'Well, that's just fine. I can tell you from now, though, that I might follow your orders at work, but don't think that I'm going to be fetching and carrying for you while we're here.'

She picked up the plate because her little speech hadn't provoked him into activity, picked up the two mugs and stormed off to the kitchen.

When she returned, hovering to look down at him, he was virtually asleep.

'I'll be heading off to bed now,' she said awkwardly. 'The spare room is first left on the landing. I haven't been in, but I presume it's made up.'

His eyes flickered open, unnervingly black and glittering in the semi-shadows. They fastened on her, sapping her and making her feel confused.

This, she thought despairingly, was what she would have to watch out for. The enemy in the camp was herself, her treacherous body which could be roused to shameful response without even being touched. She schooled her features accordingly and began to move away.

'You'll freeze up there,' he said conversationally, and she turned back to face him. 'You yourself said that what awakened you was the cold. Well, I won't be up to tend this fire and when it goes out, you'll go numb. At least down here will remain warm for much longer.'

'I'll risk it,' Abigail informed him lightly, and he frowned.

'Why?'

'Why?' She searched around for a suitable reply to that and didn't find any. 'Because,' she pointed out lamely, 'there's only one sofa down here.'

'I'll sleep on the floor. I'm sure something could be rigged up.'

'No bother.' Sleep here in the same room as him? Rig something up so that she could spend what remained of the night in a state of nervous tension, listening to his every movement? No chance.

'Fine, but don't say I didn't warn you.'

'I won't.' She turned and walked away and it was only when she was at the top of the stairs that she was aware of him behind her, taking them two at a time, his long legs covering the distance until he was standing next to her.

She edged against the wall and said sharply, 'What do you think you're doing?'

'Sheets? Blankets? You don't expect me to fall asleep like this, do you?'

The question invited her to look at him and she didn't.

'In that case, the spare bedroom is right behind you.' Her voice sounded taut in the silence and her back was pressed against the wall in the attitude of a cornered rat.

'OK.' He lowered his eyes, his long lashes falling against his cheek. 'Bit jumpy, aren't you?' he asked with soft amusement. 'What do you think I'm going to do?'

'Nothing!' Her voice sounded far too high and she cleared her throat. 'I'm not jumpy. It's just that, well, naturally, with the lights going and all that, I've been a bit rattled.'

'I thought you said that you were fine?' he asked immediately, staring at her, and she blushed, hating him for needling her into justifying her behaviour.

He could be very inquisitional when he wanted. He did it when he wanted something from someone and when the most handy tactic was to circle them like a

predator until they had nowhere to run. He also did it for amusement, and this, she thought angrily, was why he was doing it now, making her stumble over her words. In the normal course of events, at work, it was diplomatic to ignore his occasional provocation, but out here, on neutral ground, she wasn't going to keep quiet and smile a lot. She wouldn't show him what sort of effect he had on her, but she damn well wouldn't hesitate to show him that provoking her was not a good idea.

'I would be,' she said coolly, with more composure in her voice, 'if you would fetch what you came for and go to sleep.'

'Of course,' Ross murmured obligingly, looking down but not before she saw the wicked gleam in his eyes, 'just so long as you're all right and you don't twist and turn and think that I'm going to barge my way into your bedroom and rape you.'

'Difficult,' she mused icily, 'when I have every intention of locking my bedroom door.'

She turned away and he called out from behind her, 'So you *are* jumpy with me in the house!' He laughed under his breath and she knew that if there had been anything to hand she would have flung it at his smug head.

The blankets, when she made it back to her bed, were ice-cold and she huddled into a ball underneath them, teeth chattering, wishing that she had had the sense to slip on a pair of socks before jumping in.

It was earlier than she had expected. Not yet midnight, although it felt later. She lay in the darkness, eyes wide open, staring at the shadows on the walls and furniture and thinking how her peaceful little interlude had been shattered.

She couldn't face the prospect of an indefinite stay in a very small cottage with only Ross Anderson for company. Even when they had been in America, work

matters had absorbed most of their leisure time, and, she thought with some desperation, just look at what had happened when they had been together without the work to keep them occupied. Ross found her amusing. She was different from the type of women he normally dated. That was why he had made that light pass at her in Boston, a light pass which had nearly ended up wrecking her life. The fact that he already had a girl-friend had not been any deterrent.

She groaned aloud and punched the pillow in helpless frustration. He should never have come here. She should never have told him where she was going. She should have pretended to listen to his warnings about snow and told him that she was going to stay in London. Should, should, should. By the time she drifted off into a restless sleep, her head was rebounding with shoulds.

She awoke less than three hours later. The room was very cold. For a while, she lay completely still and told herself that it was mostly in her mind. She *knew* that the heating was not working, and so she *felt* far colder than she would have otherwise. She had once been told a story about a group of people locked inside a hot, cramped room somewhere on a ship. They had been collapsing from the heat when someone said that a window somewhere had been prised open. No one questioned them, they accepted it and spent the rest of the journey in relative comfort only to find that no window had been opened at all. She told herself that what she was experiencing was the same thing.

She spent another half-hour trying to persuade her body to listen to her mind, and then abandoned the struggle. The fact was that she was freezing and it wasn't going to get any warmer. Ross, damn him, had been right. The effect of the log fire was dying and there was no central heating set on timer to come on in an hour's time.

She clutched the blankets around her and tiptoed down the stairs.

Why should he sleep in comfort when she was rigid with cold?

The logs were still burning, but only just. Abigail eyed the warm rug in front of the fire greedily, then shifted her gaze to where Ross was sound asleep on the sofa.

She had no intention of waking him up. There was no way that he was going to have the last laugh. She would grab some sleep, perhaps a couple of hours, and then head back up to the bedroom before daybreak. He would never know. He was out like a light and likely to stay that way for several hours after the mammoth journey he had had.

She hitched the blankets around her tightly, to make sure that she didn't inadvertently knock against anything, and settled in front of the fire with a little sigh of relief.

For a while she listened to Ross's even breathing, her body tense in case he woke up, but sleep was weighing on her eyelids, and she could feel herself relax and begin to drift off. It was a wonderful feeling.

She was having a dream. A very vivid dream. In it, she was somewhere very hot, she could feel the sun burning down on her body, and Ross was next to her, his hands wandering over her body, his mouth against the warm curve of her neck. She could feel the pleasurable ripples of sensation touching every corner of her body, and she sighed and smiled. She twisted her position, and her eyes flew open because she was no longer alone inside the blankets. Ross was next to her.

Abigail sat up, instantly awake, and looked down at the dark, handsome face which the faint light of the moon threw into shadows and angles.

'Lie back down, woman,' he said drowsily, and she grabbed the blanket around her.

'What,' she hissed, 'do you think you're doing?'

'What does it look like to you?'

It was dark, but not so dark that she couldn't make out the dry half-smile, which sent her into a spasm of speechless fury. How dared he? His thigh was by her toes and she edged them away, curling her feet underneath her.

'Get out,' she told him in a low, angry voice. 'Back to the sofa!'

'Why?' he asked implacably. 'The cold woke me and I saw that you had decided to set up camp on the ground, so I figured that two bodies underneath the blankets would generate infinitely more heat than one.'

Abigail looked at him with dislike, remembering her dream with a shudder of humiliation.

'You figured wrong, in that case.' She yanked the blankets towards her and he pulled them back, which made her even more furious.

'*Let go*,' she demanded. 'Right. If you don't have the decency to go back where you belong, which incidentally is your own apartment in London, or at least *the sofa* while you happen to be here as an uninvited guest, then I shall just have to go back upstairs.'

She stood up and his hand snapped out, curving round her wrist and pulling her back down so that she half fell on top of him in an undignified heap.

Her heart was beating fiercely and she put her hands on his chest to push herself back up, but was thwarted by a combination of unobliging blankets, which had somehow managed to wrap themselves around her like a cage, and his arms which were infinitely more unobliging than the blankets.

They stared at each other in silence, their faces only inches apart.

'Don't be a fool, Abby,' he murmured, and the husky depth of his voice made her head begin to swim. 'You

know I'm right. This place is like an ice-box, and if we can warm each other then we might as well, because it'll do us both good to get some sleep.'

'You are the most objectionable man I have ever, *ever* met in my entire life.' The words were bitten out separately.

'Well, I guess that's better than being boring.'

She ground her teeth together and made an inarticulate, strangled sound.

'Light the fire,' she told him. 'Light the damned fire and then you can get back to the sofa!'

He didn't even bother to look in the direction of the logs. 'My body finds it far nicer to remain where it is.'

She wanted to scream.

'Relax,' he told her seriously. 'This is just a practical solution to a temporary problem.' He eased her down, applying a little pressure when she squirmed against him.

He wasn't going to take no for an answer. She lay down, with her back to his stomach, being very careful to avoid any bodily contact, and trying to ignore the warmth of his arms around her. Her head was swarming with a mad whirlwind of thoughts and she was breathing quickly and nervously. Of course, she was never going to get to sleep. She would have slept better if she had remained upstairs in the bedroom, even if that entailed her slowly freezing into a block of ice.

'Better?' he asked, and she didn't say anything. 'You're very fiery underneath that icy veneer of yours, aren't you?'

'I have no idea what you're talking about and I want to get some sleep.'

'I knew that there was more to you than what you wanted to show,' he carried on in a murmur. 'There's a lot of truth in the saying that still waters run deep. Every so often I used to catch glimpses of something quite different from the cool, efficient secretarial mask.'

'Why are you telling me this?' Abigail asked. The panic inside her was so sharp and alarming that she didn't dare move. In fact, she hardly dared breathe. 'You shouldn't be here,' she said bitterly. 'I wish you'd never come.'

'Why?'

'Because this is... wrong,' she told him. 'I work for you. I'm your secretary!' She hoped that that would put things back into perspective, but it didn't. 'You're involved with someone else,' she continued desperately. 'We've been through all this!' she virtually wailed.

'So we have,' Ross said huskily, and she was glad that he couldn't see the tremor of despairing excitement that crossed her face. 'Why are you so afraid? That boss of yours, the one you used to work for, well, you may have been attracted to him but basically I don't think you liked him very much, and you may have liked your ex-fiancé—you've told me enough times what a thoroughly warm and wonderful human being he is—but face it, you weren't attracted to him. That, in fact, may have been one of the things that you liked so much about him. Somehow, between the ex-boss and your mother, you've come to the erroneous conclusion that physical attraction between a man and a woman is somehow undesirable.'

'That's not it at all,' Abigail replied with a mixture of desperation and despair, 'that's the conclusion that *you've* come to because you feel as though you've somehow lost your challenge unless you've succeeded in psychoanalysing me from head to toe. Please,' she said in a whisper, 'won't you leave me alone?'

There was a heavy silence, then he did something that she was not expecting. He moved closer to her and folded his arms around her body, and she stopped breathing, every nerve in her body alight.

'I can't,' he muttered, not explaining what he meant.

'This won't do.' Her voice was high and pleading. This was circumstance, she wanted to tell him, this was an intimacy that had nothing to do with real life, just as Boston and what happened there had been a misjudgment brought on by being in a strange place. An abridged version of a holiday romance, she thought with scorn, the sort of thing that she had always abhorred. Foreign places, unfamiliar situations could make people lose their minds and do things which they would regret in the cold light of day. Her affair with Ellis had been cut off from reality as well. She hadn't seen it at the time, but he had made sure to point it out to her all right, the minute he thought that she might have started taking their affair too seriously. Reality had been the girlfriend from his own social stratum.

'No, it won't, will it?' he agreed, and there was an edge of excitement in his voice that raced to her brain like adrenalin and made her feel suddenly weak.

His hand moved slowly down her body, smoothing along her thigh, then slipped beneath her pyjama top, caressing the flat planes of her stomach, and she groaned with a mixture of protest and wanting.

He must know what she was feeling, he must sense the sickening intense desire inside her which was stirring into life and growing by the second.

There were so many reasons to be fighting this, and they were all clamouring inside her head, a jumble of thoughts that seemed to be locked away inside a box, audible but incoherent, uselessly warning her that every touch, every sigh, every moment of forbidden pleasure would have to be paid for in pain.

She shuddered convulsively as his hand warmly trailed down to her briefs, teasing and tantalising, and with agonised abandon she rolled over on to her back, allowing him to part her legs and then drawing in a deep,

sharp breath when he found the moist warmth of her womanhood and began to caress it.

They weren't speaking but they didn't have to. His body was giving off the same urgent messages as her own. They were both breathing thickly, their eyes locked, while their bodies obeyed orders from a different source.

She closed her eyes as his fingers explored the depth of her being, a slow, rhythmic exploration that sent darts of pleasure shooting through her.

She unbuttoned the top of her pyjamas, to reveal her aching breasts, and as he continued to excite her with his fingers, he took one swollen nipple into the warm cavern of his mouth, sucking and teasing until she couldn't bear the peak of desire to which he was sending her.

'Touch me,' he ordered her, and she did. Her ignorance of the male body was complete, and she felt his hardened member with an incredulous thrill.

He groaned and lay back and she felt the cold ache of withdrawal as he slipped off his clothes, then he roughly removed hers, his hands as impatient to continue the lingering caress of her body as hers were for his.

He knelt over her, kissing her mouth, her neck, slipping down to lick her breasts, her nipples, then lower, circling her navel, trailing downwards until she felt a spiral of intense, erotic pleasure as his hands caressed the inside of her thighs and his tongue found the hot, burning centre of her need.

She squirmed, abandoning herself to the waves of pleasure, moving against him as the waves crashed harder. When she knew that she could take no more and her body was screaming out for release, he straightened and thrust inside her, gently at first, then building to an urgent rhythm that repeated hers, so that their bodies moved as one.

She wrapped her arms around his muscled body and her legs over his and they reached the point of no return with shuddering delight.

'Ross...' she said weakly, and he placed one finger over her lips.

'Don't talk,' he murmured. He pulled the blankets over them, although she was warm enough without them.

'We can't lie here in silence indefinitely,' she said on an amused sigh. She was waiting for the guilt to come; she knew that it was there, biding its time, but right now she felt no guilt at all, just a wonderful feeling of deep contentment.

He moved to lie alongside her and stroked her hair with his hand. In the shadows, his eyes were gleaming pools. You could drown in them, she thought, if you hadn't already.

'No regrets, Abby?' he asked. Underneath the casual voice there was a hint of hesitancy and she shook her head slowly.

'Not really.'

'Is that the best you can do?'

She laughed huskily. 'No regrets.' Not yet, anyway, she amended silently to herself.

'Where do we go from here?' he asked, and she said lightly,

'To the logs? So that we can get a fire going? It'll be daytime soon.' She didn't want to discuss where they were going because she knew where they were going, and that was precisely nowhere. They might have slept together, they might have shared the ultimate bond between a man and a woman, but their paths were not parallel, and they still stood on opposite sides of a huge divide. Ross didn't want the things that she wanted out of life: he was a wanderer, a predator who never cared to stay too long in one place, while she wanted stability, needed it.

Their worlds were also light-years apart, and there was no point in kidding herself that their making love had altered that in any way. He moved in circles which she had only ever glimpsed from the outside, and when and if he did decide to settle down he would never settle down with her. That was the way it was. She had had many lessons on the nature of it from her mother over the years and Ellis had simply driven the point home.

But she hadn't been lying. There were no regrets. Later would come the time for those.

CHAPTER EIGHT

IT WAS light when Abigail next opened her eyes. The fire was roaring, and she had kicked off the blankets in her sleep. She sat up, rubbing her eyes, blearily noticing that it was still snowing. It took a minute or two before she remembered where she was and what she was doing here, downstairs in front of the fire, when she should have been upstairs in her own bed.

'Up at last, I see.' Ross's drawl from the direction of the kitchen was lazily amused, and she turned round, as memories of their lovemaking flooded back into her head.

He walked across to her in his jeans and T-shirt and handed her a cup of coffee, which she took warily, not meeting his eyes.

'I see it's still snowing,' she said neutrally, and he laughed, a low, sexy laugh that made her blood run hot.

'Is that the best you can do for conversation after last night?'

He twirled a few strands of hair around one long finger, then cupped her face with his hand.

Abigail raised worried eyes to his.

'I'm not sure . . .' she began.

'Yes, you are.'

'You don't know what I'm going to say.'

'Of course I do. You're going to tell me that you're not sure about last night, that things look different in the morning, that our lovemaking was another one of those errors of judgement which seem to be your

139

favourite excuse for anything you do that you might possibly regret.'

She smiled shyly at him. 'I'm not sure if I like what you're saying about my personality. One minute I'm an enigma, the next I'm a predictable old bore.'

'I simply know you better than you think,' Ross murmured, stroking her cheek with his thumb.

She sighed and drank some more of the coffee. In fact, she didn't know what to think or what to feel. She had given herself to him the night before, without reservations, and she didn't regret having done so, but she was too sensible to see it as anything other than a fling for him.

'You analyse things too much,' he said huskily, his eyes warm. 'You should just sit back and enjoy life.'

'Don't you mean *lie* back and enjoy it?' Abigail asked, and he grinned, bending his head to kiss her, a slow, lingering kiss that made her think that he had a point. Why ask uncomfortable questions when she could just keep silent and go with the flow?

'I should get up,' she murmured against his mouth, not moving, and he drew back to look at her.

'Why? It's still snowing, there's still no electricity, and there's no point trying to be industrious and work out some plan for leaving this place because we won't be able to. At least not yet.' He sat down on the floor beside her.

'I have to get changed,' she protested.

'You will. In due course.' He kissed her again and traced a feathery line along her lips with his tongue. While he kissed her, he began to undo the buttons of her pyjama top and she groaned in heady anticipation.

'I never thought,' he muttered a little unsteadily, 'that I could find old-fashioned, striped pyjamas so damned sexy.'

'They're not meant to be sexy,' Abigail breathed, laughing a little, 'they're meant to be sensible.'

'You don't have a very sensible body.'

He held her breast in his hand and began massaging it gently, and she tilted her head back, balancing her body on her outstretched hands behind her.

He kissed her again, and she wrapped her arm around his neck, pulling him down beside her and slipping her hand underneath the T-shirt to stroke his chest. He moaned as her hand travelled downwards and toyed across his stomach, playing teasingly against the waistband of his trousers, and she laughed under her breath.

'Enjoying yourself, are you?' he asked, breathing quickly, and she smiled.

'Wasn't that your advice?'

'You witch.' He began kissing her urgently, his mouth hard and demanding on hers. She squirmed out of her clothes and moved his hand from her breast to her stomach, opening her legs slightly so that he could explore further.

He was an extraordinary lover. She had little experience, but he made her feel as though every sigh, every little act, was giving him immense pleasure. When he guided her hand to his arousal, she could feel it throb between her fingers, against the palm of her hand, and was amazed to find that that gave her a heady sense of power.

How could she even begin to think rationally when her body was on fire and her mind was floating somewhere far above in the heavens?

He licked the full swell of her breast, then thrust deep into her, filling every pore of her being.

With a little cry of pleasure, she wrapped her legs around his body and felt his mouth crush against hers in a fierce, hungry caress.

It was an amazing way to wake up, she thought afterwards, and she looked at him through her lashes.

'What are you thinking?' he asked lazily, and she half smiled.

'What happens next.' Her voice was light and careless, but her body had tensed as she waited for his reply.

'What normally happens next between lovers,' he murmured.

'What about your girlfriend?' Abigail asked bluntly, and he frowned.

'Fiona?' There was a hint of impatience in his voice, but she wasn't going to let that send her skittering back into silence with the question unanswered.

'You have more than one?' she asked, keeping her voice light and even, and her expression as carefully uninterested as she could make it.

'There was never anything serious between us. I've already told you that.' He shrugged and ran his fingers through his hair.

'She's under the impression that you two are destined for wedded bliss,' Abigail informed him bluntly, and he burst out laughing.

'She said that to you?'

'Yes, she did.'

'Odd. Why would she say something like that to you? Well, she's wildly off course,' he said, standing up, then turning towards the fire to warm his hands. Abigail looked at the long, straight line of his back, the muscular length of his legs, the powerful forearms, and shivered with a mixture of dread and desire. Had it been stupid to have taken what she had so desperately wanted? she asked herself.

He turned to face her and she looked away, sitting up and slipping on her clothes.

'Is she?' Her voice was casual, and he couldn't see her face because she was looking down while she buttoned up the pyjama top.

'Fiona thinks I'm a good catch. I told her from the start that I'm not about to commit myself to any woman. She knew the rules of the game.' He shoved on his trousers, but didn't bother with the T-shirt, and moved to inspect the weather outside from one of the windows. 'What kind of car did you get to drive up here? Four-wheel-drive? Not that there's much chance of us going anywhere just at the moment.'

Abigail looked at him and stood up, stretching, and his eyes wandered the length of her body in open appraisal.

'Why don't you believe in marriage?' she asked conversationally, stooping to pick up the blankets and then folding them neatly, concentrating very hard on the task.

He didn't answer and when she looked up at him it was to find his eyes narrowed speculatively on her.

'It doesn't figure in my plans at the moment,' he drawled. 'Why the interest?'

'No reason.'

'You're not looking for a replacement for your boyfriend, are you?' he asked silkily, his dark face unsmiling.

'Of course not.' She felt sure that that was true, even though she had a second of doubt.

'Good.' He smiled, his lips curving, and moved across to her. 'You needn't be jealous of Fiona,' he murmured into her ear, putting both his arms around her waist.

'I'm not,' Abigail lied. 'I feel sorry for her, but I'm not jealous of her.' The accusation might be true but it made her bristle to think that he suspected her of being jealous on his account.

Ross looked down at her, taken aback. 'Why on earth do you feel sorry for her?' he asked with a puzzled frown.

'Because she thought that what you two had going was more substantial than a romp in the hay, a few meals out and the occasional present.'

She unclasped his arms and he stood back, with his hands in his pockets.

'Then I'd say that she made a dangerous assumption,' he said calmly, while she gathered up the folded linen and began walking upstairs.

When she emerged thirty minutes later, she was wearing a pair of jeans and a red and blue striped cotton jumper, and she had shoved the sleeves up to the elbows. There might not be any central heating, but the log fire was burning vigorously, and giving out enough heat to warm the cottage.

Ross was in the kitchen and he turned around as soon as he heard her coming down the stairs, his dark eyes flicking over her in a casual but intimate way. He was busy cooking on the gas cooker.

'Brunch,' he explained, watching her curious expression as she stood next to him. 'Fried bread, bacon, tinned tomatoes, fried potatoes, baked beans.'

'Sounds healthy,' Abigail remarked.

'Set the table and don't be so damned sarcastic, or I shall hand it over to you.'

Abigail laughed and began putting plates and cups on the table. Actually, it smelled wonderful and she was starving.

'I didn't think that you could cook,' she admitted to him as she bit into a mouthful of food.

'I'd hardly call this a gourmet meal,' Ross pointed out drily. 'As a matter of fact, though, I may not be brilliant at operating coffee-machines, but I'm a very able cook.'

'Are you?'

'There's no need to look so surprised. I'm an unmarried man, of course I can knock up the occasional

meal. Believe it or not, I don't spend every evening dining out.'

'There must be no end of women willing to cook meals for you, though,' Abigail said, without thinking, and he frowned slightly.

'I try not to encourage that,' he commented, staring at her over the rim of his coffee-cup. 'I don't want any woman carving out a little niche in my apartment and then thinking that she's indispensable.'

'No, of course not,' Abigail said evenly. 'Indispensable isn't a word that figures in your vocabulary, so I remember you telling me.' And even if he hadn't, she would have guessed. Ross Anderson was not a fireside and slippers man. Wasn't that why he had found Martin so dull? Wasn't that why he found the whole concept of stability so boring? He lived life in the fast lane, a wealthy, powerful man who preferred to avoid the clutter of a little woman back at the ranch, cooking supper and waiting for his return. He enjoyed women but he didn't want to be encumbered with one.

In which case, Abigail thought, what am I doing here? The question confused her.

'Should we try and see if we can clear a path out of here?' she asked, changing the subject. 'The snow doesn't seem so bad, and perhaps if we could make it to the main road we'd be all right.'

Ross stood up and came over to where she was standing by the kitchen sink. 'I'm not sure if I find the thought of leaving here all that appealing,' he said in a low voice that made her head spin.

He slipped both his hands underneath her jumper and circled her nipples with his fingers, smiling as her breathing quickened.

'Do you?' he asked, pushing up the jumper so that her breasts were exposed.

'Not when you do that,' she said shakily, looking into his eyes and seeing the reflection of her own desire. He bent to lick the erect nipples and she groaned.

'We should try and make a start,' she murmured weakly and he sighed, straightening and lowering her jumper.

'I suppose so. The snow's definitely on the way out. I'll go out and see what can be done. What kind of car have you got?'

She told him and he frowned thoughtfully. 'I'll start the engine anyway,' he said. 'Make sure that the damn thing will still go after this. If we can make it to my car, we'll stand a better chance.'

The cottage seemed disconcertingly empty without Ross in it. The cosy charm which had filled her with a relaxed glow now irritated her, and was somehow lifeless and stifling. She kept peering out of the window, watching him while he shovelled away the snow, with the steady hum of the engine in the background. The car had started up first time and, because the cottage was set amid trees, the actual fall of snow on the ground was thick, but not so thick that it couldn't be cleared, at least partially, with a great deal of work.

Abigail watched the steady rise and fall of Ross's shoulders, the grim concentration on his face. It would be strange getting back to London. She wanted to keep seeing Ross, even though she hated the dependency she was beginning to feel. It was as if he had got into her bloodstream and, now that he was there, was running wild through her, turning her into someone else. The calm, detached person had given way to someone more elemental, and that frightened her.

There's nothing wrong in sleeping with him, she argued with herself. Why shouldn't she enjoy the pleasure he gave her while she could? What would be the point in

fighting the intense physical attraction she felt for him? Would that make her a better person?

She drifted back to the sofa and tried to read, while outside the snow cleared to give way to hazy, unwilling sunshine.

It was mid-afternoon when Ross came back inside, stripping off his clothes immediately and wiping his face with his arm.

'Well?' she asked, jumping up.

'Well,' he said, 'what about some coffee and I'll deliver my progress report?'

She made him a cup of coffee, with her body on red alert now that he was back inside the cottage, and waited while he thirstily drank.

'I think we could be out of here tomorrow morning,' he said. 'The snow's stopped and with any luck that'll be the end of it, and with what I've cleared, and some thawing overnight, it shouldn't be a problem.'

'That's a relief,' she said dubiously, and their eyes met in shared understanding.

'It's not going to end just because we're no longer here,' he said. 'I'd still want you whether we were in the Lake District, London or Timbuktu for that matter.'

'I can't work for you and...'

'Why not?'

She shrugged and turned away. Now that she was facing it, the prospect of returning to reality was frankly awful. She didn't want to get back to the steady grind of London, and she could already feel an insistent voice in her telling her that what had happened between them had been madness, lunacy. For a while they had been swept out of time, but she would have to come back down to earth.

'Look at me, Abby,' he commanded, putting down the coffee-cup and turning her to face him. 'There's an electricity between us, and there's no point in pretending

that it doesn't exist. Neither of us is looking for any
kind of commitment, and we get along well together.
Why agonise about it?'

He shot her a persuasive smile, a question in his raised
brows.

When he smiled like that, Abigail found it very hard
to think straight.

'Tell me that you don't want my company and I'll get
out of your life,' he murmured, with a hint of caress in
his voice.

'It's not as simple as that,' she said, muddled. 'Martin
and I, well, I thought that he was the real thing, I thought
that what I felt for him was love.'

'Love confuses things,' Ross said bluntly. 'I've wit-
nessed enough divorces among my friends to be in any
doubt that what starts out as love ends up as bitterness.
Love is a selfish emotion and a misleading one. People
in love think that it will get them through anything, but
love and real life don't go together.'

'That's very cynical,' she said, disturbed.

'Is it? The statistics prove my point.'

'The statistics also prove that for every one marriage
that ends in disaster, there will be another that doesn't,'
she pointed out, and he shook his head impatiently.

'That's a gamble I'd rather live without.' He stared at
her and his eyes were hard and inflexible. 'If you're
looking for love, Abby, then we might just as well finish
this before it starts.'

'Is that the speech you give to all of your girlfriends?'
She didn't want him to see how much his words had
affected her. It was a silly, hypothetical conversation
anyway. She wasn't looking for love. She had too soon
ended one relationship to even think about finding
another, not that Ross Anderson would qualify as a can-
didate for a serious relationship anyway. She was in-

tensely attracted to him, but it was a purely physical thing.

'I don't want to hurt you,' he said, searching her face.

'Oh, you couldn't,' she said lightly, turning away so that his probing eyes couldn't read the expression on her face. 'You're right, neither of us is looking for commitment, and you could only hurt me if I did want something more, if I were in love with you.' She laughed and it sounded brittle. 'And of course, I'm not.'

'That's good,' he said, looking away, with a dull flush on his cheekbones.

'I still don't think that I could become your mistress, though,' she said in a low voice. 'I know that it's a bit like trying to lock the stable door after the horse has bolted, but...' She hesitated. 'I've never... I'm not promiscuous; I don't run around with men.'

'I know,' he said with an intimate laugh that made her blush.

'It would make working together very difficult.'

'Only if you let it.'

She sighed. 'Can I think about it?' she asked, even though it was more a statement of fact than a question.

He shrugged, and when he spoke there was the same teasing tone in his voice, although his mouth was hard. 'Trying to tell me that if it comes to a choice between your job or me, you'd choose the job?'

He didn't like that, she could see. Ross Anderson was not used to rejection. He had a staggering sexual appeal and had probably been bowling women over from the cradle. She doubted that any woman had ever told him that she would have to go away and think about whether she wanted involvement with him.

'It's a very good job,' she commented mildly. 'I would find it very difficult to get another one quite like it.'

He was finding it difficult not to scowl, and he changed the conversation abruptly, talking about the weather

conditions. The snow had vanished as quickly as it had come, and he told her that they would have to make a run for it, literally, as early as possible the following morning. It would be stupid to bank on clear weather indefinitely.

'What shall we do about my rented car?' Abigail asked, relieved to be on neutral ground. 'I could always follow you back to the motorway, and then return it to their head office in London,' she said thoughtfully.

'We'll see,' he replied negligently. He was keeping his distance, and she suspected that there was an element of pique behind that. He might be attracted to her, for whatever reasons, but he wasn't about to beg, and they spent the rest of the evening chatting amicably enough, but then he merely nodded when she went upstairs to her bedroom after a cup of coffee, and branched off into the guest room. The heating had returned three hours earlier and not only was it now warm everywhere, but there was also hot water, enough for a shower. There was also light, wonderful light, instead of walking around in a state of pervading greyness, broken only by candles and the glow from the fire. In a way, she missed the romantic semi-darkness, but in another she was relieved that things were back to normal. It helped. It made what had happened between them seem like a dream, and dreams were no threat to her peace of mind.

It was a slow process getting from the cottage to his Range Rover, and without much discussion they decided that she would follow him down to London. It would save him having to send someone along to collect her car.

That suited her fine. She wanted the time on her own anyway; she needed to think. Ross still hadn't said a word to her about what would happen to them once they returned to London, and she hadn't broached the

subject. Now, with the car travelling south, and civilisation reminding her at every turn that the reality that she had tried to push away in the cottage was inescapable, Abigail felt the true force of her stupidity sinking in.

She had made a grave mistake. She could see that now, in the quiet of her car, without that dark, handsome face compelling her to ignore her judgement and take what was on offer. She had learnt nothing from what had happened in Boston. She wondered whether he was similarly regretting what had happened between them.

When they got to London, with his car slowly covering the miles so that she could keep up in hers, she flashed her headlights at him twice and disappeared in the direction of her apartment.

She unpacked her bags from the car and trundled inside, and the mundaneness of the flat hit her as soon as she stepped through the front door. The dishes were still standing on the draining board in the kitchen, right where she had left them, the plants were in dire need of water, even the cushion on the sofa where she had sat before she left still bore the indentation of her body. What had happened at the cottage had been a wild fire that had raged through her system, scorching through everything, and that fire had been extinguished. Hadn't it?

Her mother called to ask her where she had been, and then, once she had established that everything was all right, spent half an hour reiterating her thoughts on the broken engagement and trying to persuade her daughter to reconsider her idiot behaviour.

'You're a fool,' she said, and Abigail could picture the pursed lips and the disapproving shake of the head. 'You'll end up on the shelf if you're not careful, my girl. Martin was right for you, a nice young man.'

'Martin was *not* right for me, Mother,' Abigail said quietly and with conviction. 'In fact, I can safely say that the best thing I ever did was breaking off our engagement. Now that's the end of that, and I don't want you ever, *ever* to bring the subject up again.'

Which left her mother speechless and by the end of the conversation obligingly subdued. Maybe, Abigail thought with a twinge of satisfaction, all my mother needed was a firm hand. From adolescent quaking, she had progressed to silence when it came to dealing with her mother, and now she wondered whether what had been needed all along had simply been forthrightness.

Martin then called to tell her that he had been worried because he and Alice had heard on the news how badly the Lake District had been affected by snow and power cuts. They chatted briefly, and she could already feel the stilted tenor of their conversation as a prelude to what would eventually come. She would keep in touch with them both, because of Alice, but visits would be polite rather than warm and no doubt eventually they would be reduced to Christmas cards with a quick note to exchange news. She didn't dislike Alice because of what she had done—after all, Martin had hardly been her property at the time, if he ever had been—but there would always be an edge of wariness in their dealings with one another. That was life.

She called the car rental company to inform them that she would be delivering the car back to London, which sent them into a paroxysm of confusion and paper rustling. By the end of the day she felt dead on her feet and depressingly defeated.

She made herself a light dinner of beans and spaghetti, which tasted fairly awful, and was about to clear the dishes when the doorbell went. She felt herself freeze. She couldn't face Ross, not yet. She had to have some time to regain her composure, and if that was him at

the door, she knew that her composure was destined to head straight through the window.

She was so convinced that it was going to be him that when she opened the door, making sure to leave the chain on, it was almost a relief to find Fiona standing outside.

'It's very cold out here,' the other woman said, when Abigail made no attempt to remove the chain.

The relief was giving way to curiosity, and she pulled open the door and stood aside so that Fiona could enter. Which she did with great presence, the self-confident, easy stride of a woman who knew that she would be noticed wherever she went.

She was wearing an ankle-length ivory coat, which would have looked ridiculous on anyone else, but which gave her an air of studied elegance that suited the tailored pale hair and the diamond-cold eyes. Abigail observed her in silence, and then politely invited her to sit down.

Fiona glanced at the chair, as if looking for germs, and then lowered herself languidly down. Her movements were all poised and graceful and Abigail observed them with dry amusement. Did Fiona ever let her hair down, she wondered, or did she even go to sleep wearing a face that looked ready to be photographed?

'I've come to see you about Ross,' Fiona said, leaning forward with one hand falling over her knee.

'Oh, yes?' Polite but wary, not giving anything away.

'I know where you were these past couple of days. Stuck up in some cottage in the middle of nowhere.' She lowered her eyes. 'I told him that there was no need for him to go on some silly rescue mission, but he had got it into his head that you needed a knight in shining armour. I told him that you already had one, in fact you were going to be married to one, and he said that that would never take place, that the whole thing had been called off.' She raised her blue eyes to Abigail's, looking for confirmation.

'Yes, it has,' Abigail said awkwardly.

'Why?' The voice was still cold and there was a glimmer of pure hatred behind the azure eyes.

'Look, what's the point in talking about all this?'

'You slept with him, didn't you?' Fiona asked, and Abigail went red. 'I knew it.' She stood up and began to pace around the room, her expression grim. 'How could you? He's mine!'

'He doesn't belong to anybody,' Abigail began, but she could hear the guilt in her voice, the admission that what she had done had been reckless and unwise. Fiona heard it too. She faced Abigail from across the room, with her arms folded.

'He'll never marry you,' she said with cold dislike. 'You're his secretary, for God's sake! He might play around with you for a while, but he'll never settle down with you!'

'I don't want to settle down.'

'Yes, you do! You're in love with him. Do you think I'm blind?'

Abigail could feel the colour drain out of her face, and she held on to the back of the sofa for support. In love with him? Of course she was. It stared her in the face and she couldn't even deny it. And all the time she had convinced herself that what she felt had been no more than attraction, a normal reaction to a man like Ross Anderson, something she wasn't particularly proud of, but something which she felt she could shrug off without lasting damage. All along she had convinced herself that she was mad to have let her guard slip, but that the spectre of Ellis Fitzmerton was enough to save her from the true insanity of falling in love with Ross.

Now, in retrospect, she could see that all the symptoms of something much deeper had been there. He had grown on her over the months: she had spent too long being a part of his life, getting to know his dry sense of humour,

the way he thought, the way he looked sitting back in his chair, dictating to her, or leaning over her to explain something. Everything had sunk into her subconscious and had taken root. She knew now what she had confusedly denied to herself, which was that she would never have made love with him if she hadn't been deeply in love with him. Martin had been a shadow which she had tried hard to make real, but he had never fuelled her the way Ross did.

Fiona smiled triumphantly. 'You're not in his league. If he were serious about you, he would have told me to get lost, wouldn't he?' Abigail didn't say anything, and Fiona continued in the same relentless voice, 'I don't know if you think you have any sort of hold over him because you shared a bed, but you haven't. You're not the first woman he's slept with. You're . . .' She searched around for the most insulting description she could think of and came up with it. 'You're comic relief, the buffoon in a Shakespeare play, for God's sake! He's already forgotten about you! Two nights in a cottage, that's all it meant to him! I suppose you threw yourself at him. The plain, desperate little secretary laying her meagre selection of goods on the shelf and begging for them to be taken.'

Abigail's legs were feeling distinctly shaky. 'That,' she said in a flat, dull voice, 'is disgusting.' Was that how he saw it as well? she wondered.

'The truth often is.' Fiona's lips curled back into a smile of active dislike. 'And on the subject of which, I found out a few little truths about you, my dear.' She paused for effect. Fiona was accustomed to pausing for effect. It was something she did very well. 'I decided to do a little digging into your past. You might send out innocent, butter-wouldn't-melt-in-your-mouth signals, but you're a woman and I know better than to believe that there's such a thing as an innocent woman. When

Ross told me that you had broken off your engagement, I thought that I'd see what I could find out about you.' She paused. 'It wasn't difficult. I rooted through your personnel file and found out the name of the company you used to work for, then I telephoned and said that I had interviewed you for a job and who could I talk to, in confidence, about your work. I said that I couldn't speak to your present boss because he didn't know that you were planning on leaving.'

'You did that? You... How could you?'

'Very easily, my dear.' Her arched eyebrows conveyed malicious triumph. 'And guess what? There was a man there who was simply dying to tell all, so to speak.'

Abigail was beginning to feel quite ill. Ellis. Dear Ellis whom she had spurned at that party a week ago.

'I met him for a drink,' Fiona said into the thick silence, 'and he was most forthcoming. With a little flattery, I managed to have a very educational chat with him.'

'Ross knows all about Ellis,' Abigail said bluntly.

'Ah, but does he know that you targeted your ex-boss because you thought that he was a good marriage prospect?'

'I never did any such thing!'

'And might he just assume, with a little prodding from me of course, that you targeted him in exactly the same way? Might he be led to think that you got engaged to that *sweet* little chap of yours because you were under the impression that he had more money than you later discovered? It's so easy, my dear, isn't it, to think that a man is made of the green stuff when he's busy courting and making the right impression? Might he, and I only say *might*, reach the sad conclusion that you broke off your engagement and decided to go back to your original target as soon as you discovered the true state of affairs with your *dear*, *sweet* boyfriend?'

'He might if he's a certified idiot,' Abigail said faintly and Fiona smiled.

'But men are, aren't they? Especially a suspicious man like Ross.'

'Get out of my flat. Now.'

'I intend to.' Fiona swept herself back into her coat. 'Leave him alone. Find someone else, someone on your own level. He's mine! If you try and come between us, I'll make sure that you regret it. I'll tell him a thousand lies if I have to and he'll believe them because there will be just enough there to sound like the gospel truth.' She smiled a cold, hard smile. 'That's a promise. I've told my friends, my family, that Ross Anderson is the man for me and he will be.'

Abigail looked at her with pity. 'Will be?' she said scathingly. 'Maybe we're both chasing windmills.'

Fiona walked across to the door, her expression ice. 'I,' she said, 'at least have a chance.'

She pulled open the door and slammed it behind her, and Abigail remained where she was, then slowly regained her strength and began clearing away the dishes. She had a bath, she changed, she brushed her hair, but she felt dead inside.

She didn't want to think about what Ross meant to her. Every time the awful truth reared up in her head, she swept it aside until she got tired and gave in, and thought and thought until she felt her mind would explode.

All her adult life she had carried around the idea that love was safe and that safety was desirable, the one solid thing in a changing world. She had been a plain child, she had grown into a pleasant-looking but by no means beautiful woman, and she had had it instilled in her from an early age that happiness was finding someone on her own level. Ellis had been an exercise in finding out that painful truth, and when Martin had come along her brain

had logically worked out that he fitted that description, and she had never considered the possibility of being stupid enough to reject that in favour of her boss, the one man whose easy charm and lazy sex appeal she had observed from the sidelines, thinking herself happily immune.

The only glimmer in what was a disastrous scenario was that Ross didn't know that she loved him. That would have been the most humiliating thing that she could have imagined. Fiona, after only meeting her a couple of times, had guessed at the truth, but then women were often more intuitive than men.

She wondered what Ross's reaction would be if he ever found out how she felt. Amusement, perhaps, then maybe a certain amount of wariness. He had warned her that love and marriage were not for him. If he even suspected for an instant that she had fallen in love with him, he would turn his back and walk away as quickly as he could, and that would be without Fiona's version of truth-telling.

Fiona, she thought, was very optimistic if she imagined that she had the wherewithal to net him, but then there were always two sides to a story and Ross, intent on seduction, would hardly have told her that he was planning to marry another woman. She didn't see him as capable of such deceit, but Fiona was determined, available and socially suitable, and many a man had capitulated for less. She was also dangerous and scheming.

The thoughts played through her brain over and over, until she finally fell into exhausted sleep and went in to work the following morning feeling zombie-like, but strangely calm. There were no more cobwebs in her mind, no more nagging doubts; the jigsaw puzzle was all in place. She loved Ross Anderson, it was a hopeless situ-

ation, and from that starting point everything she did could only go uphill.

She pictured the tunnel stretching in front of her, one in which there would be no more of him, no more surreptitious glances at his handsome, angular face which she knew as well as her own, no more rush of adrenalin whenever he was around. It was bleak, but she told herself that she could get over it. Time cured everything, didn't it? Loving him was crazy and hurt like hell, but it wasn't terminal.

She walked into her office, relieved to find that he hadn't yet arrived, and sat down at her word processor. Then she switched on the screen and typed out her letter of resignation, which she folded into an envelope, and placed on top of his desk. He couldn't miss it.

When he walked into the room an hour later, she looked up at him, smiled politely and then waited for the summons to come.

CHAPTER NINE

SHE waited half an hour, then an hour, and finally, when he did call her into the office, she was too nettled by his lack of response to feel apprehensive. Had she thought that she was so important in his life that he would hit the roof when he opened that little white envelope? On a personal front, Fiona had been right, Abigail thought bitterly. To Ross, she was little more than an interesting interlude, nothing to get worked up about. And on a work front, she might be a good secretary, but good secretaries were two a penny.

She looked at him calmly and then sat down on the chair facing him without a word.

It was only now, now that she had admitted her love for him to herself, that she realised how accustomed she had become to seeing him. For months she had watched him from a distance, storing up everything about him without even noticing that she was doing so. There was an awful lot that she would have to relegate to memory, and that filled her with a brief but painful sense of despair, but she kept her face blank, waiting for him to speak.

He had her letter in front of him, and he took it between two fingers, holding it as though it were something he had fished out of the bin, something a little unsavoury.

'I take it that this is not a joke?'

'No, it's not,' Abigail agreed tonelessly. The way his thick black hair sprang back from his face, that was something she would have to forget.

'Fine.' His voice was cool. 'You'll have to get to work on recruiting your replacement.'

That hurt. She hadn't expected a flood of emotion, but this didn't even qualify as a light shower.

'Of course,' she said in a low voice. 'I'll be in touch with the employment agencies today, unless you'd like to recruit someone from inside the company.'

He shrugged and looked bored. 'It's all the same to me, just so long as she can do her job.'

'I know Mary who works in the sales department has been looking for a change.'

'Mary? Who's Mary?'

'She works for Mr McGregor's team,' Abigail said, and he nodded.

'The blonde one with the legs?'

'That's right.' Her throat was threatening to seize up but she faced him with a bland expression.

'Just make sure that that's not all she comes qualified with. I don't want someone whose only asset is looking ornamental.'

'Of course not. I'll set up an interview for this afternoon.' She stood up and he leaned back in the swivel chair and fixed her with icy eyes.

'Sit back down.'

She sat back down, feeling nervous and miserable. She knew him well enough to know that he would never let himself become dependent on anyone. The true strength in any company, he had once told her, was to ensure that no one was irreplaceable. Valuable, yes, but not irreplaceable. Why should she have felt that her departure meant more to him than a temporary inconvenience?

'I take it,' he said coldly, 'that you intend to explain why I came in here this morning to find your letter of resignation on my desk?'

'You know why,' she said quietly.

'Oh, but I want you to tell me, face to face.'

'Very well. I don't see how I can work efficiently for you after what's happened between us.'

'We made love and now you think that I won't be able to keep my hands to myself, even though you want to put it all behind you?'

'No, that's not it,' she stammered, and he gave her a humourless smile.

'No? Then please elucidate. I'm dying to hear.'

'When you asked me, when you said that we could...' She faltered and he bared his teeth in another smile.

'Have an affair?'

'I told you that I would think about it, and I have. I've decided that I couldn't. It would be wrong for me.'

'Fine, that's your prerogative, but I still don't see what that has to do with whether you leave or stay. Not unless there's something that you aren't telling me?'

He stood up and strolled across to the window and absentmindedly stared down before turning to face her.

'Something like what?' This is it, she thought, he's going to inform me in that way of his that I've fallen in love with him, and I'm going to shrivel up in embarrassment.

'Let's put it this way.' He leant forward against the desk, propping himself up, and stared at her with hard eyes. 'When Plan A with your ex-boss failed to net you the marriage you wanted, and Plan B failed because your ex-boyfriend wasn't liquid enough for your liking, did you decide that Plan C, to slot me in the winning post, was the next best thing? Only to discover that I was rather more reluctant to be drawn into marriage than you had expected?'

Her eyes flared angrily. 'That is the most despicable thing I have ever heard in my whole life!'

She stood up and he roared, 'Sit back down!'

'I suppose you heard all that from your girlfriend?' Abigail said bitterly. 'Just as I suppose you won't believe a word I say if I try to deny it all?'

'Feel free to deny.'

'None of it's true. You know why I left my last job.' She looked at him defiantly, but there was a tell-tale flush on her cheeks. 'I was wrong about Ellis, but I never wanted to marry him for money! And as for Martin— don't you think that I might have guessed that he was short of cash from his job? He hardly came to fetch me from my flat in a Rolls-Royce!'

'And what about me?' he asked softly. 'Did you think that you could get me to marry you? Did you believe that sleeping with me would put a ring on your finger?'

When she replied, her voice was icy and controlled. 'I was a fool to sleep with you,' she said, 'and no, I never considered marriage at the end of it. I might have been a fool, but I would have had to be certifiable ever to expect that for an instant.'

She should have known that Fiona would never have uttered empty threats. She had run to Ross with her devious little fabrications and she had been right. Nothing about any of the accusations rang true, but there was just that little thread of possibility which would have stirred his suspicions. Suspicions were impossible to fight, they were too nebulous. It was like trying to get hold of a cloud.

'In that case, why the sudden urge to leave? Do you think that you're so irresistible that I would make your life here hell?'

'That's not fair,' she said unhappily, and he looked away, a dark flush spreading over his face.

'I told you once that I never beg. Not for you or for any woman. Whether I believe what Fiona said or not is irrelevant. Did you think that by handing in your resignation you might provoke me into fighting for you?'

'It was the last thing on my mind,' Abigail replied truthfully.

'Of course, you know that you'll never find a job as good as this one, or as well paid,' he said coolly, and she nodded, fighting down the urge to burst into tears.

'Something will come up. Would you want me to work out my full notice?' she asked, hoping not. Her full notice was six weeks and she didn't know whether she could face him, every day, for six more weeks. Just sitting here now, looking at him, thinking about how much she was going to miss his sometimes arrogant, sometimes volatile, sometimes charming, always intelligent, company, made her go numb.

'I damn well would,' he informed her, leaning forward and linking his fingers together. For the first time she caught the glimpse of anger behind the cool mask, and it didn't really surprise her. 'Don't think,' he said in a smooth, cruel voice, 'that you can run off because you've suddenly decided that it's become too uncomfortable here for you, whatever the bloody reason. You're not about to leave this office in a state of chaos because of something personal.'

'I would never do that,' she protested, meeting his eyes. 'I would make sure that my replacement was fully trained before I even thought of going.'

'Which should take just about the length of your notice, don't you think?'

She stood up. 'Is that all?' she asked, and he nodded, looking down at the work on his desk and waving her away with a dismissive gesture.

He knew how to hit where it hurt most, she thought, walking back to her desk. He wouldn't give her, or any woman, she suspected, the satisfaction of showing a display of raw emotion. He didn't need anyone and he had made the point as bluntly as if he had posted a sign on her desk telling her so.

She telephoned the sales department later that morning, and told Mary that her position was becoming vacant, and would she like to apply for the post? By mid-afternoon, she suspected that her resignation would be public property within the company, and by the following afternoon every other branch throughout the country would have heard. In an office, news travelled like wildfire, especially news that had to do with the boss. She wondered what sort of speculation would circulate as to the reasons for her departure, and decided that she didn't care. She was on friendly terms with a few people within the organisation, but not so close that she would have been offended by their curiosity.

Ross emerged at lunchtime and told her in a distant, curtly polite voice that he would be away for the rest of the afternoon. He gave her a list of things that needed to be done, and then left, without a backward glance.

She read everything into his remoteness. It remained with her for the rest of the day and preyed on her mind. Ross Anderson was telling her, without having to spell it out word for laborious word, that their brief passionate encounter meant nothing to him, and that her decision to leave was one that wasn't going to upset his world. He was also telling her that if she had even been thinking of commitment with him, then she had been living in cloud cuckoo land, and that was a bitter pill to swallow because it was the one thing she had known all along, right from the very first moment when her attraction to him crept out into the open, and still she had plunged on, still she had given herself to him.

She went into work the following day, to find that Ross's cool, polite manner was still there, freezing her out, reminding her of his indifference. He barely glanced in her direction and when he did his eyes rested on her with the courteous blankness of a stranger. He still gave orders, but his voice was restrained, and when she

brought Mary in to see him she got the feeling that replacing her was a technicality which he saw as only a
minor hiccup.

She could have become used to the remoteness if she
had never known the shared familiarity, if she had never
seen the man behind the power. As it was, the week
dragged past in an atmosphere of calm which had her
feeling exhausted by the time Friday rolled around.

She wondered what had happened to Fiona. She hadn't
seen the other woman or taken any calls from her at
work, but that didn't mean that Ross had not returned
to her, and the thought of that ate away inside her. Was
she still prodding away? Insinuating in that sly way of
hers? Hardening suspicions?

Two weeks after she returned from the cottage, and with
only four left to go before she was released from the
painful captivity of working for Ross, Abigail remembered the company Christmas party. The Christmas
parties, which were usually held in one of the grander
of the London hotels, never took place at Christmas.
Over the years, most people had come to view them as
the working version of a spring ball. Abigail herself had
arranged the location, the food and the venue, but that
had been months back, and she had completely forgotten about it until she opened her desk diary and found
the reminder staring her in the face.

Of course, she would have remembered if she hadn't
been consumed with her own problems. She would have
heard other employees chatting about it, but she had
been moving and working in her own little isolated world,
battling with her emotional problems, and the party had
been the furthest thing from her mind.

She sat at her desk that evening, waiting for Ross to
emerge from his office, which he did, and he looked

across at her with a mixture of mild surprise and casual indifference.

'I've been meaning to have a word with you,' Abigail said, standing up as he moved towards the door to leave. He inclined his head politely, pausing with one hand on the doorknob, waiting for her to say what she had to say.

'It's about the Christmas party on Friday,' she began uncomfortably.

'What about it?' Distant, civil, his dark eyes expressing little beyond restrained curiosity. Every time he looked at her like that, she felt as though a knife were slicing through her.

'I'm afraid it completely slipped my mind, and I won't be able to come. I've made other arrangements.'

'You'll have to cancel them. You're my personal assistant and you are expected to attend.'

'I don't think that it would matter very much whether I attended or not,' Abigail retorted, her voice rising. 'I'm due to leave in four weeks' time!'

'I will expect to see you there,' Ross informed her in a flat, icy voice that left no room for argument. He looked at his watch. 'Is that all or was there something else?'

'Nothing else,' she said, pitching her tone to match his, and he nodded and left. She looked at the closed door with a tide of emotions rising in her: anger, hurt, bitterness. She wanted to scream at the invisible wall of silence that stood between them, even though she knew well enough that without that wall of silence there would still be a wall between them, but a wall of a different sort.

Damn him, she thought angrily, why shouldn't I go to this Christmas party? Why should I change my life because of him?

The following afternoon, in a spirit of angry rebellion, Abigail left work early and spent three hours wandering through the shops, looking for that elusive dress that would raise her morale and show Ross Anderson that whatever had happened between them had had no effect on her, that she was as indifferent to it all as he was.

She found the perfect outfit in jade-green. It had a high neckline and long sleeves, but it was close-fitting and seemed to hold a great deal of bold promise. She tried it on and it made her feel good anyway, so she bought it, spending far more than she had anticipated.

Ross was not around the following day. Abigail arrived at work very early, cleared a great deal of paperwork, in between trying to show Mary the intricacies of the filing system, and at four-thirty they looked at each other with a conspiratorial smile.

'It is the party tonight,' Mary said with a giggle, 'and we will only be leaving an hour early.'

'Are you trying to corrupt me?' Abigail asked sternly, but she had already decided that she would leave early provided she cleared her desk.

'I need to spend quite a bit of time on my beauty routine if I'm to look presentable.'

Abigail looked at her wryly. 'I find that hard to believe.'

Mary was tall, leggy, and with the sort of good looks that came from an attractive personality as well as an attractive face. She smiled a lot and, underneath the blonde hair, was good at her job and willing to work hard.

Abigail tried not to think too hard about Ross, working with her replacement, building up the rapport which they had shared for so long and which had become the bitter bedrock of her life. It didn't do to dwell on

those things. It made her see too clearly the empty chasm stretching out in front of her.

She would have to leave by seven, and she had a leisurely bath, washed and dried her hair, considered doing something daring with it and then decided against the idea, and finally changed into her outfit, which felt even more glamorous with the appropriate accessories than it had in the shop. She would never be a raving beauty, but she intended making the most of what she had: her trim figure, her neat features.

What a laugh even to imply that she would try and net a man for his money. With my unremarkable face, she thought, it would be quite a ridiculous notion. But Fiona hadn't seen that. All she had seen was a face that had managed to get Ross Anderson into bed.

There were already quite a few people at the ballroom by the time she arrived, faces that Abigail recognised, some well enough to speak to, others known only by sight. She didn't look around for Ross. She allowed herself to meander from group to group, chatting amicably about her resignation, about needing a change of scenery, vague small-talk that wouldn't raise eyebrows but would kill any seeds of curiosity which might be in the process of germination.

She heard Mary's voice before she saw her. It was a distinctive voice, deep for a woman, with a hint of laughter in it.

'There's Abigail! Abigail! Over here!'

Abigail swung round and saw Ross long before her brain had registered the people to whom he was talking. He was in a superbly tailored dinner jacket and one hand was in the pocket of his trousers, while the other was holding a glass. She didn't want to look at him, but it was very difficult. In any group, he was always the centre of attention. For a start, he was usually taller than

everyone else, but also he had an air of vitality that made it hard not to focus on him.

She edged politely into the group, and out of the corner of her eye she could see him watching her twisting the stem of the champagne glass in his hand.

Mary, ebullient as ever, was holding court, while her boyfriend, a quiet, sandy-haired man, who looked older than he probably was because of his receding hairline, smiled and looked vaguely uncomfortable.

During a pause in the conversation, one of the sales managers turned to her and said, smiling, 'So, have you found another job yet, Abby?'

'I thought I might have a month off work before I get anything fixed up,' she said. She liked James Davies. He was in his forties, a calm, affable family man who inspired hard work in his staff without having to demand it. His wife, plump, with blonde hair and an easygoing disposition, was standing next to him, listening politely to their exchange. Abigail tended to meet her at office parties, as she did most of her colleagues' partners.

'Recovering from that slave-driving boss of yours, eh?'

Abigail nodded politely and looked at Ross, who stared back at her with biting intensity. Everyone else seemed unaware of any tension in the atmosphere, but she could feel it, it was there in the hardness behind the black eyes.

'You're bound to miss it, though,' Mary said, grinning. 'You can't work for someone for all that time and not miss it when you leave.'

'There are lots of things I shall miss about the company,' Abigail agreed non-committally, and Ross said, in a hard voice that was masked by a polite smile, for the benefit of everyone else,

'But I'm sure Abby will bring her great talents to whatever job she takes up.' He drank the rest of the champagne and stared at her with a savage little smile. 'You do enter fully into your job, don't you, Abigail?

I'm sure whoever you work for will find that an enormous benefit.'

Abigail smiled stiffly back at him.

'I certainly hope so, Mr Anderson,' she replied in a sweet, syrupy voice. Her eyes glazed over and she looked around her with the stiff smile still on her face. James and his wife drifted off in the direction of some of the sales crew, and the little group began breaking up, the way they tended to at office functions.

'Drink?' he offered before she could similarly slink away, and she shook her head without looking at him.

'If you don't mind,' she said politely, 'I think I might do the rounds. There are a lot of people here whom I won't see again and I'd like to say goodbye.'

'But I do mind,' Ross said, and she looked up at him with acid surprise.

'Do you? Why? Do you want to subject me to a few more insults while you have the opportunity?' Her mouth twisted and she smiled even though it hurt. 'Why don't you circulate as well? Then you could tell everyone what great talents I'll be taking to my new job, how much my new boss will be impressed with them!' Her voice had started out full of biting emotion but she ended on a whisper.

'Well, won't they?' he bit out. 'You had a damned affair with your ex-boss and you slept with me——'

'I never slept with Ellis!'

'Where's the difference between us?' he ground out, ignoring her anguished interruption, twisting the stem of his glass in his long fingers.

'This is pointless,' she said, forcing herself to smile as a group of acquaintances walked past and waved at her.

'Not to me, it isn't.'

'What do you want from me?' she asked tightly, knowing that he was pushing her towards the awful con-

fession that what she felt for him was second to none, and backing away from any such confession for dear life.

'Oh, God,' he said fiercely, raking his fingers through his hair.

'It's over. Why bother to do a post-mortem on it? Let's just say that our relationship, if that's not too exaggerated a word for it, died of natural causes.'

He started to say something, his face savage, but it was an impossible place to talk. There were too many people swarming around them, too many eyes glancing in their direction, and he was as aware of that as she was. This crowd, which would later ruthlessly look for reasons behind her departure, were, for the moment, her allies, giving her cover, protecting her from a conversation she couldn't cope with.

She called out to someone passing by and any snatched privacy they had had was lost.

Later, over dinner, she felt her eyes drifting to his stiff back, speculating furiously on what was going on in his head. He had been cold and offhand with her in the office but now there was barely concealed fury in him.

From the round table where she was sitting, with seven other people, she glanced at him from under her lashes and tried to make polite conversation with the people around her.

After the meal there was a disco. Everyone drifted out of the room so that the tables could be cleared away, breaking up into natural groups of friends, and for a while she lost sight of him altogether.

When she next saw him, back in the dining-room which was now dimly lit and crowded with people, some dancing, others standing around and chatting over the music, she got a shock. He wasn't alone. He was on the dance floor with Fiona. She had not been there for the meal but she must have arrived on the scene shortly after.

Abigail looked at the figures on the dance floor and felt a sick feeling wash over her in a tidal wave.

One of the men who worked in the sales department meandered over to her and, from what seemed a huge distance away, she heard him ask her to dance. He was smiling and waiting and not expecting to be turned down. Abigail knew him well enough; she knew most of the sales department pretty well because she dealt with them all so regularly, and she knew that Gary Chalmers was very fond of himself, so she made a light quip about his harem and how was it that he could fit her in, and received the expected chuckle of self-congratulatory modesty.

She rested her head on his shoulder and closed her eyes, while Gary's chatter swam around her and all she could think of was Ross and the ache in the pit of her stomach. When the music ended, she straightened and looked up to find him staring right at her. Let him think the worst, she decided recklessly. She kept one arm around Gary's waist and the music continued with another slow song. She thought of Ross and Fiona, their bodies like one, she thought of him whispering into Fiona's ear, his breath like a warm tickle on her face, she imagined what he was whispering, and felt her heart constrict.

She was so miserable that she was hardly aware of her feet keeping step with Gary's. She was hardly aware when people began leaving. Ross, in keeping with his position, would be the last to leave, and Fiona would doubtless be at his side, declaring to the world that they were an item.

Poor Gary, she thought after a while, four straight dances in a row when his harem was patiently waiting.

She moved to join a group of girls, secretaries like herself, and when it seemed a decent enough time to leave, she stood up and made an unobtrusive exit.

There was a mass of people queueing at the cloakroom and she looked at them with a sinking feeling. Then, rather than join the queue and be obliged to contribute to the raised voices and high laughter, she went across to one of the chairs which had been pushed against the wall and sat down. She felt incredibly weary.

'I thought you might be here,' a voice said from over her, and Abigail looked up. When most people were beginning to look a bit tattered at the edges, Fiona still managed to look glamorous and impeccably made up. Didn't that sleek tailored blonde hair ever become dishevelled? Abigail looked at her with dislike and wished that she would just go away.

'I didn't expect to find you here. I thought that you might have had a bit more pride, but then I hardly expected you to be still working for Ross. I thought that you might have found that an untenable position, but then types like you hang on until you're physically thrown overboard.' Fiona wasn't looking at her. She was staring around with a bored expression, her mouth pursed and discontented. In ten years' time, Abigail thought, she would have the lines of a woman who was never satisfied with life, not that that afforded her a great deal of satisfaction.

'You're wasting your little digs on me,' she said without emphasis. 'I won't be provoked into a slanging match with you over anyone, so why the hell don't you flap away and find another victim for those vampire teeth of yours?'

A spasm of fury crossed Fiona's face and she gave Abigail the full brunt of her glacial blue eyes.

'I told Ross about you,' she said. 'But I can see it didn't work or else you wouldn't still be cluttering up his life and his office, so there's something else I want to say to you, and if you feel anything for him at all, you'll listen.'

'Go away,' Abigail repeated with restraint.

'You wouldn't want to see him dragged through the mud, would you?' Fiona asked coldly. 'I've booked a room in the hotel for the night.' Her mouth curved into a feline smile. 'I thought Ross might appreciate not having to take a taxi back to his apartment. Perhaps we could continue this conversation there? It would be infinitely more private.'

'What do you mean, dragged through the mud?' Abigail asked, and was granted another reptilian baring of the teeth.

'I thought so. In love enough to care for her man's reputation even when the man in question wants nothing further to do with her. Touching.'

'If Ross wants nothing further to do with me, Fiona,' Abigail pointed out reasonably, 'why are you making such a big fuss? Why are you trying so hard to make sure that I'm no longer around?'

The controlled reptilian smile splintered into a look of rage.

'I think we need to have a little chat, my dear,' she said. 'I think you need to find out exactly what's on the line if you don't clear out.'

'Oh, very well,' Abigail said between her teeth, because the last thing she wanted to do was cause a scene here and they were heading rapidly in that direction.

They both left, walking quickly and silently towards the lift, then along the richly carpeted corridor to Fiona's room. It was small but exquisite, with tastefully decorated walls and a great deal of antique furniture which was thoughtfully positioned to make the most of a limited amount of space. There were no clothes anywhere, no sign that the room was occupied apart from a Louis Vuitton holdall on the bed.

Fiona didn't bother to close the door. She left it ajar and strode into the room, turning to face Abigail with her hands on her hips.

'I've been watching you,' she said venomously, keeping her voice low. The upper classes, Abigail thought irrationally, never raised their voices when they argued, did they? They conducted rows in the hushed tones that people normally used in libraries. 'When I heard that you had decided to leave Ross's company, I thought that I would be rid of you, but I watched you tonight, and I'm not a fool. All that cheek-to-cheek dancing, just where Ross could see you. Do you think that I wasn't aware of the little game you were playing?' There was hatred in the eyes and the curl of the mouth.

'What game?'

Fiona laughed and there was an angry, uncontrollable edge to the laughter. 'You're still trying, aren't you? Still trying to get him, never mind the fact that I told him all about you and your manoeuvring. Well, it won't work.'

'You lied to him.'

'Yes,' Fiona agreed, 'I lied, but all's fair in love and war.'

Abigail was beginning to revise her opinions on the upper classes and their noise levels during an argument, because Fiona's voice was rising steadily, as was her colour.

'You're wrong about——' she began, but she didn't get very far.

'He was annoyed to see me there this evening! Furious! He told me that it was all over between us, and it's all your fault!' She took a step forwards and Abigail thought, Help! She eyed the half-open door with a strong desire to run.

'I'm sure you're wrong,' she murmured soothingly, which was the wrong approach.

'Don't patronise me! You might think that you're clever, leading him on with a little lovemaking, coming here tonight with your coy smiles, but you're not. You're just making a complete fool of yourself!'

'You're right,' Abigail said nervously. 'I was, am, whatever. I really must leave now.'

Fiona ignored her. 'I want you to tell Ross once and for all that whatever you had between you is finished. I want you to leave the company immediately! Ross will come back to me once he's rid of you! I know it.'

'And if I don't?' Abigail asked, fed up with being threatened, fed up with the accusations, in fact fed up with just about everything.

'If you don't,' Fiona said, taking another alarming step towards her, 'I'll make sure that his career is ruined. I'll go to the Press with all sorts of things about him, and the name I use will be yours. You'd be surprised at how greedy newspapers can be when it comes to destroying someone as eligible and successful as Ross Anderson. Especially the less scrupulous newspapers. So you'd better back off, or else I'll feed them stories that will——'

Neither of them heard approaching footsteps, but then the thick carpeting would have muffled the sound anyway, and they were both so intent on the drama taking place between them that Ross's voice from the doorway was as unexpected as a roll of thunder on a bright summer day.

'That will...? Stories that will do what, Fiona?' He strolled into the room and smiled at Fiona, a cold smile that sent a sudden chill down Abigail's back. 'I'm all ears.'

Fiona was staring with him with the stunned look of someone who had suddenly found a snake curled in the folds of her dressing-gown. Her face was white, her mouth parted in an exclamation of wordless surprise.

'I'm waiting,' Ross said conversationally, his voice silky but his eyes hard like granite.

She closed her mouth and edged backwards, then she began to stammer nervously. 'You didn't believe all that, did you, darling?' She hazarded a smile but what emerged was the shaky caricature of one. 'I only said that because... because I was prompted into it by her.'

'Her' had stepped back and was trying to fade into the background.

'Really.' Ross moved closer to Fiona's white-faced figure. He looked dark, dangerous and quite terrifying. 'Carry on. You've already done a fine job of explaining how you lied about Abigail. You have yet to inform me what exactly you were going to tell the Press about me and I'm waiting with bated breath.'

'Nothing! I told you, it was all for effect. I wouldn't do anything like that to you.' Her voice was sinking fast to a whisper and Abigail almost felt sorry for her.

'I wish I could believe you.' He shook his head sadly, but his eyes were still like granite. 'But kiss-and-tell stories are so popular with the newspapers, aren't they?'

Fiona had been rendered speechless. There was a thick silence, during which Abigail cleared her throat and said that if they didn't mind, she would be on her way, that her coat and her escort were probably getting restless.

Fiona didn't even glance in her direction, and Ross looked at her briefly and said, 'You're not going anywhere.'

He reverted his attention to Fiona, who looked as though she would dearly have loved to make a bolt for the door, but couldn't because he was blocking the exit.

'You disappoint me, Fiona,' he said, strolling towards her and smiling as she cringed back against the wardrobe in the corner of the room.

'Don't blame me,' she defended. 'I only did it because I thought we had something going, something that that

woman was intent on destroying!' That seemed to ignite
a spark of self-righteous anger, and she clung to it as a
drowning man clung to a lifebelt. 'I know you told me
that you weren't interested in settling down, but we got
along well together, and *everyone expects us to get
married*!'

'You thought that I was a fish worthy of being caught.'

'What's wrong with that?' Fiona demanded defensively. There were two bright patches on her cheeks and
the cowering was slowly being replaced by outrage.
Outrage that she was having to justify herself to him,
outrage at being sneered at. She was a woman who had
probably got her own way with men from the minute
she stepped into adolescence, and she was not accustomed to having to fight for anyone.

'Plenty,' Ross said economically.

'There are a lot of men who would give an arm and
a leg to have me!' she stormed furiously, still, Abigail
noticed, being very careful not to get too close to Ross.

'Fine. They're welcome to you.'

Her mouth thinned, but she still dared not move too
close.

'I would have made you a perfect wife,' she said
through bared teeth. 'I'm beautiful, I'm clever. You don't
think that that——' she shot a brief, scathing look at
Abigail '—nobody will do anything for you, do you? A
secretary! Not that I believe for an instant that you intend
to marry her! But if you think that I was out to catch
you, then you'd better be careful, because she——'
another jerk of the head in Abigail's direction '—has
marriage on her mind and you're blind if you don't see
it. I may have lied about her past but it was no lie when
I told you that she's after you!'

The speech, spoken so quickly and with such heat that
the words tripped over one another, was a huge error of
judgement. Ross walked towards her and when he spoke

it was slowly, clearly, and in a voice that would reduce the strongest person to a quivering wreck.

'I won't ask you to apologise to Abigail for that slur on her character,' he said, and Fiona looked at him with the resentment of a woman spurned. He gripped both her arms. 'Because,' he continued in a voice that could cut glass, 'an apology from you would be worth very little. But I'll give you a little word of advice, Fiona. We're finished and we were finished a long time ago, whether you choose to accept that or not. I suggest you get on with your life, and——' he paused and gave her a humourless smile '—don't even think about going to the Press or anyone else with stories about me, because that would make me very angry indeed. You wouldn't like to see me angry, would you, Fiona?'

'Believe me, you've seen the last of me,' she said cuttingly, taking time off to throw Abigail a look of malicious spite. 'Go to the Press? You're not worth it. You and that *secretary* of yours!'

'I feel sorry for you, Fiona,' he said acidly, and she gave him a look that could have frozen a charging bull,

'Don't, I won't leave here heartbroken, believe me. Oh, yes, I fought for you, but I fought because you were a good catch. Rich, good-looking, confident. There are other rich, good-looking, confident men out there, though, so don't think that I shall hibernate and pine over *you*.'

'Poor Fiona,' he mocked, although Abigail could hear a certain sadness in his voice, 'unable to love. Never mind money, that's one thing no amount of cash can ever buy for you.'

Fiona didn't answer. She turned to Abigail and said coldly, 'You got him. Well, enjoy him while you can, because if *I* couldn't hook him, then you, my dear, don't stand a chance in hell.'

'Run along, Fiona,' Ross said and this time the rage in his voice was all too apparent, 'you are beginning to try my patience.'

And she did. Very quickly, slamming the door behind her, and Abigail said into the silence, with some incredulity, 'This is her room!'

'So it is,' Ross agreed, turning to look at her.

Her emotions, which had been in a state of suspended animation while Fiona had been in the room, now returned with full force, and she said in a small, desperate voice, 'Well, I think I'll be getting along myself.'

'Oh, no, you don't,' Ross murmured, moving over to her. 'You're not running out on me this time.'

His face was grim and she looked at him nervously.

'I wasn't about to run out on you,' she began; 'it's just that...'

'Just that what?'

'Just that I'm tired and——'

'I don't care if you're about to drop. I have a few things to say to you and I intend to say them.'

'Why? What's the point of all this?' She moved and he stepped forward so that he was standing in front of her.

'I'm in no mood for games, Abby.'

'Nor am I! So why don't you leave me alone? Haven't you done enough? You don't own me, you know!'

'I do, you know.' His voice was husky and she looked away, not trusting herself to keep hold of her emotions. 'Is that why you walked out on me?' he asked. 'Because of Fiona?'

'Of course not!'

'Was tonight the first time that she'd warned you off me?'

'No,' Abigail said reluctantly, glancing at his taut face from under her lashes. 'But that's not why I ended our relationship.' She laughed and it was a dry, bitter sound.

'I suppose you'd like to believe that, wouldn't you? But it isn't true.'

'Look at me when I'm talking to you,' he told her roughly, catching her face with his fingers and turning her to face him. 'Tell me, then.'

'There's nothing to tell. I left because I wasn't interested in having a fling.'

'Don't stop there, Abby,' he said softly. 'Finish that thought and tell me what more you want from me and why.'

They stared at each other in thick silence and she could feel the pounding of her heart going like a hammer in her chest, making her breathless and light-headed.

'Do you have any idea what I'm going through?' Ross asked harshly and she didn't answer. 'I've been going mad, thinking about you.'

Abigail didn't say anything. She didn't want to hear this, she didn't want to rise on a tide of hope only to be thrown back down to earth.

'Say something, damn you!'

He shook her and she broke out bitterly, 'There's nothing to say! I still won't have an affair with you!'

'I'm not asking for an affair!' he snarled, and she looked at him, startled.

'Then what are you asking for?'

He turned away and raked his fingers impatiently through his hair.

'Don't you know?' he said, with his profile to her. 'I'm in love with you, Abby. I don't know when it happened, I just know that when you told me that you were engaged to a man I felt as though my foundations were collapsing.'

'Aren't you going to look at me when you talk to me?' she asked, and he faced her.

'Marry me,' he whispered unsteadily. 'Tell me that you love me.'

'Of course I love you,' she said simply, her eyes shining, and she slipped her arms around his waist. She felt as though she was coming home, returning to a place where she belonged.

His arms tightened around her and he kissed her, his tongue exploring her mouth, then he buried his head against her neck.

'When I first saw that man I felt sick. I didn't have to turn up at your engagement party, I didn't want to, but something was driving me on. I got there with Fiona complaining all the way, and it was like being punched in the chest. I felt betrayed!' He laughed shakily under his breath. 'I needed you! How could you just decide to marry someone without... without... ?'

'Asking your permission?' she teased.

He shot her a dark, brooding look, then lifted her off her feet and carried her to the sofa, sitting down with her on his lap.

'We can't do anything here!' she protested, and he ignored her.

'Of course you should have asked my permission!' he told her.

'And what would you have said?'

'Not to be damned stupid. You see, little by little I'd come to depend on you. Do you know that unconsciously I compared other women to you?' He made a rueful sound. 'You'd managed to edge your way under my skin and when I spoke to another woman, I kept saying to myself that *Abigail* wouldn't be so stupid, so lacking in self-irony, so conceited, so weight-conscious. I didn't even realise what was going on. Then I found myself looking at you, thinking about you. I'm not sure when I started wanting you, but suddenly I felt as though I'd been catapulted back into adolescence. Every move you made fascinated me.'

'You were seeing Fiona!' Abigail reminded him.

'No, I wasn't. She was seeing me. I broke it off with her shortly after that disastrous engagement party, but she refused to accept it, and I suppose, for a while, I felt sorry for her.'

He pulled her towards him and their lips met, as his hand stroked her thigh, found the lacy edge of her stocking and caressed the bare flesh above it.

'I never loved Martin,' Abigail said softly. 'We met and something clicked. Friendship, I guess, and we both mistook friendship for something else. We were both so ripe for falling in love. He was desperate to settle down, to start a family, and, well...' She paused reflectively. 'I suppose I thought that the stability he offered was what I was looking for, especially after what I'd been through with Ellis. I hadn't been in love with Ellis, but it was still a blow when he laughed at what we had.' She sighed. 'When you told me that he wasn't the man for me, I was angry, because I had had niggling doubts of my own. I just wasn't sure.'

She settled against him, leaning her head on his shoulder. He eased her dress up, and she squirmed, giggling.

'We really mustn't. What if Fiona comes back? Her bag's still on the bed!'

'So it is,' he murmured. 'Well, I'd better see to that, then, hadn't I?'

He lifted her and placed her gently on the bed, then made a brief call to Reception. The room was now occupied. The lady who had booked the room might return for a bag, in which case they were to tell her that the bag would be forwarded to her address. Abigail could hear them murmuring consent down the line. Power and wealth pulled strings, and Ross was well known enough to the hotel for no fuss to be made. The owner was a personal friend of his, and the staff treated him with the respect reserved for only a privileged few.

Then he went to the door and slipped the chain across. She watched his movements with languid fascination. She still couldn't believe that this proud, arrogant man was in love with her. She felt deliriously happy. How could she ever have imagined that what she felt for Martin had been anything substantial? Love was pain and ecstasy, anguish and needing.

'Better?' he asked, sinking on to the bed next to her, and she nodded.

'It's been hell, you know,' he murmured, 'in the office. Watching you. Wanting you. Hating myself for still wanting you when you had told me to get lost. When you told me about that man in your last job, I felt sick. How could I fight your preconceptions of me? Then when I saw him at that party, I could have strangled him. I'd never been jealous of anyone in my life before, and suddenly I was feeling murderous towards two perfect strangers just because they happened to have been close to you somewhere along the way. I wasn't going to show you how much you'd winded me when you told me that you weren't going to have an affair with me. I thought that I was being a fool, that if I could treat you like a stranger, then whatever chaos was happening inside me might go away. I was crazy.' He began unbuttoning his shirt, and when he had disrobed to his boxer shorts he said with restrained passion, 'I want to see you undress. Slowly. My own personal striptease. I seem to have been waiting for so long.'

The only light in the room was the glow from the bedside lamp. Ross had switched off the top light, and Abigail, with blushing self-consciousness, stood up and began wriggling out of her dress.

'Slowly!' he commanded, and she felt a pulse of excited delight as she looked at his dark eyes, drowsy with desire.

She removed her dress, slowly, and he smiled, then she undid her bra and cradled her breasts in her hands, with a wicked, thrilling lack of inhibition. When she reached to unfasten her suspenders, he told her not to, so she removed her briefs instead, then joined him on the bed, closing her eyes as he trailed his hand along the length of her body.

'You're exquisite,' he murmured. 'You have a body that should never see the inside of an office suit again.'

'I don't think that would be wise, do you?' she asked with a gurgle.

'No,' he agreed. 'It's for my eyes only.' He smoothed her thighs, then began caressing her with the flat of his hand, and she half closed her eyes, moving against him.

'I couldn't bear the thought that other men had kissed you. Before then, women were pleasant companions but never more. If any one of them had told me that she had found someone else, I would have shrugged and wished her the best luck in the world. That's why I couldn't understand my rage when you told me that you were going to marry that man. And after we spent that time in the cottage in the Lake District.' He paused the steady rhythm of his hand and cupped her face. There was raw emotion in his eyes. 'God, woman, it was as though I had never known the meaning of making love! Then you told me that you weren't sure, that you'd have to think about it.' He drew in a sharp breath. 'What was there to think about? I couldn't conceive that you didn't feel the same as I did.'

'I loved you,' Abigail said soberly. 'I couldn't bear the thought of being hurt by you. Don't forget I'd worked with you; I'd seen you close up and I knew your track record.'

'It wasn't good, was it?' he said in a rueful voice and she laughed.

'I've known better. But I wasn't about to become a casualty. Love makes you vulnerable.' She sought for the words. 'Besides, we were so different. I was an ordinary working girl and I'd always had it drummed into me that I was destined to marry a good, ordinary man. The first time Fiona warned me off you, she told me that we were from different worlds, and part of me was willing to believe her because it was something that frightened me as well. When Ellis and I broke up he laughed in my face, you know. I don't think he meant to be unkind, not deliberately, but he found the thought of us having some sort of serious relationship quite ludicrous, and since I'd spent a lifetime hearing that sort of thing from my mother, having it drummed into me that I was an average girl who should expect an average life, I believed him.'

'That bastard,' Ross said. 'But shall I astound you? I am a good, ordinary man. Money doesn't make you into a villain. And I love you so much, no one will ever be able to offer you more stability and security than I will.'

He kissed her neck, and his mouth continued its melting caresses along her body.

'You never told me,' he said under his breath.

'Told you what?'

'That you'd marry me.'

'Maybe I should think about it,' she said thoughtfully, then she laughed. 'Or maybe there's no need to state the obvious.'

Coming Next Month

HARLEQUIN PRESENTS®

THE BEST HAS JUST GOTTEN BETTER

#1833 THE FATHER OF HER CHILD Emma Darcy
Lauren didn't want to fall in love again—but when she saw Michael all her good resolutions went out the window. And when she learned he was out to break her heart she vowed never to see him again. But it was too late....

#1834 WILD HUNGER Charlotte Lamb
Book Four: *SINS*
Why was Gerard, famous foreign correspondent, following Keira? She could hardly believe he was interested in the story of a supermodel fighting a constant battle with food. No, he wanted something more....

#1835 THE TROPHY HUSBAND Lynne Graham
(9 to 5)
When Sara caught her fiancé being unfaithful, her boss, Alex, helped pick up the pieces of her life. But Sara wondered what price she would have to pay for his unprecedented kindness.

#1836 THE STRENGTH OF DESIRE Alison Fraser
(This Time, Forever)
The death of Hope's husband brought his brother, Guy, back into her life, and left her with two legacies. Both meant that neither Hope nor Guy would be able to forget their erstwhile short-lived affair.

#1837 FRANCESCA Sally Wentworth
(Ties of Passion, 2)
Francesca was used to having the best of everything—and that included men. The uncouth Sam was a far cry from her usual boyfriends, but he was the only man who had ever loved her for what she was rather than what she had.

#1838 TERMS OF POSSESSION Elizabeth Power
Nadine needed money—and Cameron needed a child. His offer was extraordinary—he would possess her body and soul and the resulting baby would be his. But the arrangements were becoming complicated...

MILLION DOLLAR SWEEPSTAKES
AND
EXTRA BONUS PRIZE DRAWING

No purchase necessary. To enter the sweepstakes, follow the directions published and complete and mail your Official Entry Form. If your Official Entry Form is missing, or you wish to obtain an additional one (limit: one Official Entry Form per request, one request per outer mailing envelope) send a separate, stamped, self-addressed #10 envelope (4 1/8" X 9 1/2") via first class mail to: Million Dollar Sweepstakes and Extra Bonus Prize Drawing Entry Form, P.O. Box 1867, Buffalo, NY 14269-1867. Request must be received no later than January 15, 1998. For eligibility into the sweepstakes, entries must be received no later than March 31,1998. No liability is assumed for printing errors, lost, late, non-delivered or misdirected entries. Odds of winning are determined by the number of eligible entries distributed and received.

Sweepstakes open to residents of the U.S. (except Puerto Rico), Canada and Europe who are 18 years of age or older. All applicable laws and regulations apply. Sweepstakes offer void wherever prohibited by law. Values of all prizes are in U.S. currency. This sweepstakes is presented by Torstar Corp., its subsidiaries and affiliates, in conjunction with book, merchandise and/or product offerings. For a copy of the Official Rules governing this sweepstakes, send a self-addressed, stamped envelope (WA residents need not affix return postage) to: MILLION DOLLAR SWEEP-STAKES AND EXTRA BONUS PRIZE DRAWING Rules, P.O. Box 4470, Blair, NE 68009-4470, USA.

FAST CASH 4032 DRAW RULES
NO PURCHASE OR OBLIGATION NECESSARY

Fifty prizes of $50 each will be awarded in random drawings to be conducted no later than 11/28/96 from amongst all eligible responses to this prize offer received as of 10/15/96. To enter, follow directions, affix 1st-class postage and mail OR write Fast Cash 4032 on a 3" x 5" card along with your name and address and mail that card to: Harlequin's Fast Cash 4032 Draw, P.O. Box 1395, Buffalo, NY 14240-1395 OR P.O. Box 618, Fort Erie, Ontario L2A 5X3. (Limit: one entry per outer envelope; all entries must be sent via 1st-class mail.) Limit: one prize per household. Odds of winning are determined by the number of eligible responses received. Offer is open only to residents of the U.S. (except Puerto Rico) and Canada and is void wherever prohibited by law. All applicable laws and regulations apply. Any litigation within the province of Quebec respecting the conduct and awarding of a prize in this sweepstakes may be submitted to the Régie des alcools, des courses et des jeux. In order for a Canadian resident to win a prize, that person will be required to correctly answer a time-limited arithmetical skill-testing question to be administered by mail. Names of winners available after 12/28/96 by sending a self-addressed, stamped envelope to: Fast Cash 4032 Draw Winners, P.O. Box 4200, Blair, NE 68009-4200.

Free Gift Offer

With a Free Gift proof-of-purchase
from any Harlequin® book, you can receive
a beautiful cubic zirconia pendant.

This stunning marquise-shaped stone is a genuine cubic
zirconia—accented by an 18" gold tone necklace.
(Approximate retail value $19.95)

Send for yours today...

compliments of ◈ HARLEQUIN®

To receive your free gift, a cubic zirconia pendant, send us one original proof-of-purchase, photocopies not accepted, from the back of any Harlequin Romance®, Harlequin Presents®, Harlequin Temptation®, Harlequin Superromance®, Harlequin Intrigue®, Harlequin American Romance®, or Harlequin Historicals® title available in August, September or October at your favorite retail outlet, together with the Free Gift Certificate, plus a check or money order for $1.65 U.S./$2.15 CAN. (do not send cash) to cover postage and handling, payable to Harlequin Free Gift Offer. We will send you the specified gift. Allow 6 to 8 weeks for delivery. Offer good until October 31, 1996 or while quantities last. Offer valid in the U.S. and Canada only.

Free Gift Certificate

Name: _____

Address: _____

City: _____ State/Province: _____ Zip/Postal Code: _____

Mail this certificate, one proof-of-purchase and a check or money order for postage and handling to: HARLEQUIN FREE GIFT OFFER 1996. In the U.S.: 3010 Walden Avenue, P.O. Box 9071, Buffalo NY 14269-9057. In Canada: P.O. Box 604, Fort Erie, Ontario L2Z 5X3.

FREE GIFT OFFER   084-KMF

ONE PROOF-OF-PURCHASE

To collect your fabulous FREE GIFT, a cubic zirconia pendant, you must include this
original proof-of-purchase for each gift with the properly completed Free Gift Certificate.

084-KMF

HARLEQUIN  PRESENTS®

PRIVATE & CONFIDENTIAL

MEMO

To: The Reader

From: The Editor at Harlequin Presents

Subject: —our six sizzling stories
         of office romance!

When Sara caught her fiancé being unfaithful,
Alex, her boss, helped pick up the pieces of her
life. But Sara wondered what price she would
have to pay for his unexpected kindness....

P.S.#1835 THE TROPHY HUSBAND
      by Lynne Graham

P.P.S. Available in September wherever
      Harlequin books are sold.

You're About to Become a *Privileged Woman*

Reap the rewards of fabulous free gifts and benefits with proofs-of-purchase from Harlequin and Silhouette books

Pages & Privileges™

It's our way of thanking you for buying our books at your favorite retail stores.

PROOF OF PURCHASE
HP-PP161
Offer expires October 31, 1996

Harlequin and Silhouette— the most privileged readers in the world!

For more information about Harlequin and Silhouette's PAGES & PRIVILEGES program call the Pages & Privileges Benefits Desk: 1-503-794-2499

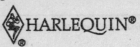

HARLEQUIN®

HP-PP161

CATHY WILLIAMS is Trinidadian and was brought up on the twin islands of Trinidad and Tobago. She was awarded a scholarship to study in Britain, and went to Exeter University in 1975 to continue her studies in the great loves of her life: languages and literature. It was there that Cathy met her husband, Richard. Since they married Cathy has lived in England, originally in the Thames Valley but now in the Midlands. Cathy and Richard have two small daughters.

Books by Cathy Williams

HARLEQUIN PRESENTS
1413—A POWERFUL ATTRACTION
1502—CARIBBEAN DESIRE

"You're a~~~~~~~~ Are~~ ~~~~"

Ross trailed his finger along her spine and Abigail's body went rigid with tension. "I have more sense than to be attracted to you!"

"What has sense got to do with it?" An odd look flickered in the depths of his eyes.

"Everything," she stated calmly. But her spine still tingled from his touch, and she realized with horror that Ross knew precisely what effect he had on her....